the hourglass man

the
hourglass man

A Novel about a Psychiatrist's Breakdown

by CARL TIKTIN

 **ARBOR HOUSE** *New York*

*To my psychoanalyst, Dr. Stephen B. Payn,
whose loving practice of his art
helped me to go from nowhere to somewhere,
and who wants it made perfectly clear
that he is not the model for the main character
in this book.*

the hourglass man

chapter one

DR. Donald Norton closed his eyes and took a deep, bracing breath before he opened the door for his new Friday 3:15 patient.

This is not Patty, he knew. She will not be there as she was last week and all the other weeks, perched tensely on the waiting room chair. He will not lead her into his office and close the door and they will not face each other, gauging each other's states and kissing accordingly . . . one week tenderly, one week passionately, one week anxiously or not at all.

This will be a new patient. A new experience. What Patty is doing is what she ought to do.

But just before he opened the door he concocted a little

episode of Patty arriving at the office in her usual time slot, miraculously knocking this new person out of the box, as it were, and sitting in the chair—dressed, as she had been last week, in faded Levi's and a plaid work shirt with no bra... more aggressively accessible to him than ever before.

He opened the door and the new woman patient rose from the chair and said, "Oh, Dr. Norton, I'm Carmelita McKay. I am so glad to see you! I know you can help me."

Her voice had a soap opera throb that he felt must be some sort of act; but as he began to look over the rest of her he knew that this must be the way she really was going to talk. She had hair on the bottom of each of her three chins except the main chin, which possessed a cleft of unmistakable classical clarity. Her lips were fixed in a nervous social smile exhibiting uneven teeth, streaked with zippy hot pink lipstick. Curiously, though, the nostrils, with little insectlike hairs protruding from them, were at the end of an almost perfect movie-starlet nose, which led to eyes that were filled with a kind of ready-to-worship-wide-eyed I-want-you-to-be-my-God-at-this-very-instant look.

And Norton could see that from the moment she saw him she had decided she had found her God.

Him.

He didn't need that now.

Goddammit, not now! It's bad enough you're not Patty but goddammit, don't be this! Nevertheless, he motioned to her to step into his inner office, and as she walked in front of him through the open door he started to take note of his new patient. He took in the unwashed black print dress; the cheap purple sweater with one button missing and the others placed in the wrong holes, streaked with what looked like mustard and ketchup; bulbous toes overlapping dirty sandals; and sagging breasts.

She turned to him when she was half way in the room and said in a gurgly little-girl voice, "Oh, what a lovely office."

4

He motioned to her to sit on the couch but she ignored his motion and moved closer to him.

"Oh," she said, "you look just like a psychiatrist should look." He hurriedly sat in his chair, and she walked to the couch and sat on it. He noted how deeply the pillows of the couch sank as she sat down. Patty had seemed to float on the pillows of his couch, as if riding the crest of a wave.

Carmelita adjusted herself to her new seat and modestly pulled her skirt over her kneecaps. Patty had done the same thing, but what a difference. The image of Patty chastely arranging her dress over her knees and then pressing her legs tightly together as if to deny that they were two separate limbs with an area between brought him sharp, painful emotions that he had to cut off in order to concentrate on the barrage of material now being launched at him about the reasons this new patient was seeking psychiatric help. She was talking about her problems, which ranged from wanting to commit suicide to just plain loneliness. She had so much to give, so much love locked in her heart, but there just did not seem to be anyone around fine enough to receive it. She knew that she wanted a meaningful relationship but was afraid to extend herself.

Norton was having increasing difficulty concentrating on what she was saying. An enormous sadness began to engulf him, and her voice was being driven out by its force. He fought by refocusing on what she was saying. He heard her talk about her office job and the fact that she studied acting at a school in the Village. But he started to drift again as she talked about her family background.

He didn't know what was wrong with him, but it almost felt as if *he* were going to cry!

He had just missed something important that she said. Someone drank. Who was it? Mother? Father?

Dammit! Come on, Donald, he told himself, let's get with it.

5

Now she was talking about overeating (God, she was all over the place!). Even as a child, she was saying, she needed love. She recalled that she used to eat as much as possible when her father (ah, yes, it was her *father*) was away drinking at a bar. She knew she weighed a bit more than she ought to but she felt that her major problem was that she couldn't seem to do anything about it.

"Do you think it's emotional, doctor?" She was asking him a direct question that required an answer and he had almost missed it.

"Have you had a physical check-up, Miss McKay?" he asked.

"Yes, I have, doctor. Everything is fine—I'll give you the name of my doctor if you'd like. Oh, one thing . . ."

"Yes?"

"Would you mind calling me Carmelita?"

He really could not sit there any longer. This enormous sadness was beginning to blur his vision and deaden his hearing. It was crazy but he really felt he was about to cry.

He stood up quickly and said, "Excuse me," damning his voice because it was weak and without substance.

He hurried toward the oversized closet on the other side of the office. As he reached the door Carmelita said, "I hope everything comes out all right."

She thought he was going to the bathroom!

He couldn't get into the closet fast enough.

Once there he leaned against the door, trying to get some objective view of what was happening to him. Ridiculously, it really did seem that he was going to cry. The muscles and passageways of his eyes, nose and throat were all geared up to produce tears. He breathed and swallowed hard to counter the accelerating forward motion of the crying apparatus. He put his hands to his eyes and closed them as if to shut off and push back any such nonsense that might try to get through. He held his breath and pressed the sides of his nose until the teary feeling subsided.

Could he go back in now?

Would he be all right?

He had never experienced this kind of thing in his entire life. Come on, Donald, shape up, fella!

He almost laughed at that. He of all people ought to know that you could not just exhort a depression to go away.

Was he having a depression?

He had never had a depression in his life! Now that he was forty, was everything going to start?! He "listened" to his body. The heaviness; the pain in the right thigh, neck, around the chest; lack of focus; difficulty in breathing; almost compulsive tears—yes, he decided, a depressive reaction. The tears were coming again. He fought them back as he had done before but they were stronger now. He felt the wetness around his eyes and he swallowed hard.

His hand reached out and grasped one of the shelves to steady himself, and he touched some antidepressant pills on the shelf—free samples left by a drug company. They were mint green and very cool looking—very tempting for a moment.

No, goddammit, Donald! I am a psychiatrist who is in his own analysis and I am not going to let chemicals do the job that I am most capable of doing!

He looked at his watch and estimated that he had been in the closet about four minutes. He would give himself another six minutes to get himself together. He could make up ten minutes, and if not he would tell Carmelita that he was ill and couldn't continue.

Idiot! he screamed at himself, you've never done that with a patient. Stupid head doctor, can't you control your own head?!

Don't be so hard on yourself, Donald, he countered, anyone would have this kind of reaction when you compare what you used to have at Friday 3:15 with what you've got. Remember your so-called objective notes on Patty after her first session: Carefully groomed young lady who in spite of rather hot weather is as covered up as she can get away with; tightness around eyes and mouth suggesting deep inner struggle, perhaps to keep the flirtatious little girl imprisoned and let the play-acting mature young lady dominate; has not looked doctor directly in the eye since coming into the office—only sideways, somewhat flirtatious glances (which engendered happy hopeful feelings in the doctor, who had never been able to have a girl like this when he was younger—and here was one totally awed by his presence—of course, the doctor would have to work this out—see her as a patient—but for now, just for now, he could let himself indulge in this fantasy a bit); high-pitched squeaky voice reflecting little-girl–mature-young-lady conflict; sits on edge of couch as if ready to spring off at a moment's notice in case she is attacked; long black hair, very luxurious; well-developed bust that she carefully tries to hide in a white page boy blouse; alert; tense; defensive; and very pretty.

His reactions made sense to him now ... there was an emotional click that comes when something hooks up. He had formed a Patty habit, and what was happening now was not a depression but a withdrawal symptom. Nothing more and nothing less, like getting off a drug or stopping smoking. Donald, you idiot, you should have known this would happen, the system forms a pattern—Patty-Friday-at-3:15 every week for many months and if the pattern is broken—boom! the system gets screwed up. All right, system, listen. She'll be back—this is just a stage she is going through and I approve of it, I really do. She needs to feel that she is independent—okay, but don't worry, she'll be in touch. Maybe it won't be at the same time, in the same place and in the same way, but you have to learn to adjust to differences, for God's sake! Okay?

He really didn't feel very much better, but at least he didn't think he would break down. He put his hand on the door knob to go out when something within the system

8

asked, What if she doesn't get in touch? What if this is the end?

The compulsive sobs started again.

No.

Goddammit. No!

She has to get in touch, he suddenly realized, looking at the reason right there in front of him on the shelf. She needs tranquilizers. She must be running out by now and she will need some new ones or a prescription. . . .

I'm sure she's made no psychiatric connection up there in Connecticut yet. If she doesn't call me I may call her . . . offer to see her and give her some pills or a prescription . . . yes, something could be worked out. . . .

He was feeling better . . . getting in control of himself. . . . the sadness was breaking. Was it because of the idea of being in touch with Patty again? No, he didn't think so, because he had always known he would see her again.

No, he was able to analyze himself and work through this feeling on his own . . . yes, that was why he was coming out of it . . .

He removed a handkerchief from his pocket and wiped his eyes, looked at his watch and observed that he had been out only about six minutes. He was ready to go back in.

There was a soft, persistent tap on the closet door. "Oh, Dr. Norton . . . Dr. Norton . . . are you all right?" Carmelita was saying as she tapped.

He was furious.

The nerve of that fat bitch—he hadn't been in there six minutes—she had no right to do that! Listen to her: "Oh, Dr. Norton, are you all right?" She disguises her anger at being left alone and her curiosity as to what he was doing with a show of overwhelming concern, he noted.

Well, fuck you, fat-ass! I'm not going to treat you. The way I feel about you it wouldn't do you any good and it certainly wouldn't do me any good . . . especially now.

He opened the door quickly and had the satisfaction of seeing a trace of fear on Carmelita's face as the door swung open. "Miss McKay," he said.

"Carmelita," she corrected.

"Carmelita," he said, "never do that. I always give my patients their full time. Any interruptions are for a good reason."

"Oh, I'm sorry, doctor. I was just worried."

He pointed to the couch in cold fury and Carmelita turned around and walked back in, with him following her. For a panicky moment he imagined he was being led. But as soon as they reestablished their respective positions by sitting down he felt secure again.

Except he had said, "Never do that," which had a definite future connotation . . .

Well, there wasn't going to be a future, he vowed. Whom should he refer her to?

Goldberg. He would refer her to Goldberg. Goldberg had time.

He concentrated easily on the material, relaxed in the knowledge that he was not going to have to deal with it beyond this session but attentive so that he could give his best diagnosis.

What would he tell Goldberg about why he was referring this patient?

No time. He would tell him that he was booked up. . . .

But no . . . he had spoken to him last week and had mentioned that he had some open time . . . besides, it's degrading to lie. Why couldn't he tell Goldberg the truth? They had been friends since their Creedmoor days. They had laughed together at obnoxious patients and doctors alike.

"Hello, Goldberg . . ." he could picture himself saying on the phone, "please take this one off my hands; I can't stand her . . . she revolts me, so help me God. Please . . . I will bless all the tribes of Israel for you, please . . ."

But Goldberg would laugh. "Donald, my boy," he would

say, "normally I gladly would do a buddy a favor, but I would be depriving your analytical mill of grist. Your analyst would have me up on charges for aiding and abetting an act-out. Remember, in analysis you don't dislike anyone, you only overreact to them."

They had also laughed together over the ritual and dogma of analysis, Norton remembered. And now Goldberg could not refrain from chiding him about analysis every time they talked.

He would send her to someone else . . . he'd think of some-one . . .

"We have to stop now," he said.

She stopped abruptly with a hurt I'm-a-little-girl-who-has-just-been-slapped look. He imagined her hand reaching for the fudge cookies, being slapped by a parent with a ruler.

"What do you think, doctor? Do I need psychotherapy?"

He decided he would tell her that he had no time available. But she would puff up with anger. If you had no time, why did you see me in the first place? Something came up, he would reply weakly. What do you mean, something came up! Are you going to charge me for this? No charge . . . no charge . . . he would say. No charge? What's the matter? Don't you value your own services, *doctor?*

She would be a tidal wave of wrath and he would sink more deeply into his seat, thinking, You are doing something wrong! Something wrong!

"What do you think, doctor?" Carmelita repeated. "Will psychotherapy help me?"

He cleared his throat. "Yes . . ." he said, "I think it can."

"I would like to come three times a week. I have insurance at the office that covers it mostly. I need three times a week."

"Twice," he said, "twice a week is all I can take . . . all the time I have now."

"Oh no . . . I need three times a week . . . please, doctor . . ."

"Twice," he snapped off at her. "Twice a week, Wednesday and Friday at this same time."

"Oh, doctor, please," she continued. "Please fit me in for three times a week..."

"Our time is up now," he said to her, standing abruptly to signal the end of the session.

She paused a moment, then quickly stood up. He led her to the door but just before he opened it for her she said, "Dr. Norton, I just want to say one thing. Your strength and firmness are just what I need. I know you are the doctor for me. I feel such a wonderful rapport in just our first session."

He nodded blandly and she left.

He found himself sitting limply at his desk.

Well, he told himself, that was the best thing I could do under the circumstances. It really would have been inappropriate not to treat this patient. Besides, I've had worse in my day. I'm beginning to miss Patty... it's natural, I know, and it'll soon pass, because I'll hear from her, but it's a fact anyway, and I mustn't make judgments based on deprivation feelings. Yet haven't people like Carmelita always bugged me? That means that there is something in me that is reflected by her. That happens to all of us, doesn't it? I mean, from time to time I bet that has even happened to you.

Who am I talking to?

Claude, my analyst, of course.

And of course Claude would say that we ought to work these feelings out so that they don't get in the way. Well, all right, Donald, he decided as he prepared to lock up the office, I'll mention it in this session coming up. I wonder if Claude will try to hook my feelings about Carmelita into feelings about my mother. Carmelita is nothing like Mother. He smiled as he thought of his delicate, dark, slender, neat-looking mother. The exact opposite of Carmelita. Oh, of course if Claude knew about Patty—which he never would —then he would have an analytical ball hooking that up. There are many superficial resemblances—coloring, a certain delicacy; and of course there are exact opposite characteristics—Mother's low voice and Patty's high squeaky one. And so on. But of course Claude would make a great deal out of the opposite characteristics too, wouldn't he? He laughed out loud. Analysts can connect anything with anything any time through any means. Life is simpler at any bar where truck drivers and steel mill workers might hang out. What if I said to the boys at the bar, Hey, you guys, you shoulda seen what came into my place today—I got this fat, horrendous hippopotamus, dirty, sloppy broad and at the same time of day that I used to have this gorgeous little dish that I was havin' a little thing with.

What did you do? they would all ask.

What do you think? I told Miss Instant Pollution to get the hell out and see me after the bath water rolls off your hide and when the fumigation machine finishes with your clothes . . .

Good for you! the boys would roar, slapping me on the back and buying me a beer.

What about the little dish? one of them would ask.

Oh, the little dish'll serve herself up again . . .

Plenty of roars, gulps of beer, leers and lewd hand gestures . . .

You see, Claude, no counter-transference discussions here —no misconceptions that just because you are a psychiatrist you have to learn to love everybody! Carmelita is disgusting and I was disgusted! Patty was beautiful and I was moved! I am not going to talk about this Carmelita thing in my session! I want to work on reconstructing the rebellious attitudes I had in my senior year in high school. Well, maybe I'll mention it . . . I'll see how it goes.

As Norton was locking the door to his office, a little thought, like a bird flitting through the branches of a tree, commented, But you didn't throw her out, did you, Donald? And Patty hasn't called yet, has she?

He gave it no weight.

chapter two

NORTON pulled his car into the driveway of Claude's summer home. He had made good time, so he was early, and he sat there a moment looking at the large old country house. No one was to be seen. He got out of the car and strolled aimlessly, trying to allow the quietness of the country to invade the buzzing electric tensions in his head and body.

He suddenly wanted to see the pond again. Did he have time? Yes—at least ten minutes before his session. He started down the road.

When Norton had first started seeing Claude up here for the summer he had walked down the road one day before an appointment and had come upon a pond at the side of the road. He was caught in its quiet grip. Almost immediately he decided that the pond to him symbolized Claude. It was a round, unobtrusive little pond, just as Claude was a rather unobtrusive short older man. The awe-inspiring thing about both was that while there was no striking, blaring activity on the surface, there never was stagnation either —only a magic mixture of vitality, alertness and peace. The pond was mysterious because its force and sustenance came from a deep invisible spring that flowed with apparent ease. He had searched to find how the water remained pure but could not find the source of the flow, just as he could not ferret out Claude's source.

He had gone into analysis more or less as a lark. The thing to do when one has established his practice and made enough money. Give the old Freudian shit a dabble—why not?

But he had stayed in to become like this, somehow—deep, peaceful, yet vibrant. He did not know how that might happen and somehow really didn't think that it would, but as long as there was a chance . . . a possibility, he ought not to ignore it.

He came upon the pond suddenly at the side of the road. It was there as it was always there—suspended in time and space, only for him. The large green leaves on its surface were in the same place they always were . . . the reflections of the surrounding trees casting the same glazed pictures they always did . . .

He walked slowly to the edge, not at all minding the mud that leapt over the sole of his shoes onto the bottoms of his pants. He intently scanned every inch of the pond, seeking to find the slightest clue, the smallest ripple, revealing the source of its flow. There was none and he really did not expect there to be any.

He bent down and touched the water, putting his wet hand to his cheek. It felt warm . . . disappointingly ordinary. Yet he knelt there quietly, as if in prayer.

When he finally rose he noticed with some small annoyance that his knee was smudged with mud. He wiped the mud off his pants with his handkerchief.

You really should work this pond thing out, dammit. Are you a secret water worshiper?

He looked at his watch and saw that he had less than a minute before the start of his session. He walked back quickly, before Claude could look out and see the car in the driveway and wonder where he was. Would Claude ask him where he had been? No, of course not; psychoanalysts never do that. I would; but, of course, I'm not an analyst, and I am free to go beyond those rigid rules ... still, Claude did make that observation last week about my not dealing with my present life ... was that pure analysis? No, I don't believe it was ... is he getting eclectic in his old age? Should I question him on it? No, I'd better not ... don't want to get him huffy. Norton reached the house just in time and rang the bell. It was promptly answered by Claude and they walked to the back of the house where Claude had set up an office.

Norton spent most of the session, free of any tension, easily associating the feelings he'd had as a senior in high school when he was sixteen with early infant memories; making connections between his fantastic ability to remember almost everything he heard or read in school, thereby getting effortless "A's," to a feeling that he always wanted to break a beautiful vase in his mother's house: seeing it smashed to pieces at Mother's feet and reveling in the shriek that would escape from her lips—she loved that piece of crockery madly. He had wanted to fail all his tests as a senior and not go to college. Once he had deliberately not studied for a biology test; but then when the test was given he saw with a combination of relief and despair that he knew the answers anyway. So he had not failed that test.

Then pretty little Eileen Shanahan came to his mind.

"That's funny," he said, interrupting his other associations, "I just had a picture of a girl I haven't thought about in at least twenty years—Eileen Shanahan . . ."

Norton became sad again—the way he had become at his office before.

"Why did you think of her?" Claude asked.

"I don't know. She was part of those times."

"How?"

"I wanted her so badly. She was very pretty, very Irish . . . map of Ireland kind of face . . . freckles . . . cross between her breasts. She was the subject of many a good masturbation."

Talking about Eileen held the sad fog within him suspended for the moment.

"What stopped you from having her?"

Norton chuckled. "I don't think I ever said two words to her. She was one of 'those' girls."

"Those girls?"

It sounded to Norton as if Claude had forgotten the careful reconstruction of his mother's attitude about civil service workers' daughters that Norton had spent God only knew how many sessions on. When he said " 'those' girls," Claude should have hooked in immediately.

"You know," Norton prompted. " 'Those' girls."

Silence from Claude.

He's forgotten, Norton knew it and was furious. Shouldn't an analyst give a prorated refund to the patient for all forgotten material, Claude? I forget nothing and I'm not even an analyst.

Would you like me to prompt you further, Claude?

Remember how Mother did not want me to get involved with a civil service worker's daughter because I'd fall in love young and marry one and start raising a family at nineteen and start taking tests for the fire department or like father, the Transit Authority and just like Bill Simms or Joe Bowie, two promising lads who could have been engineers or doctors, wind up as beer-bellied nothings instead of going to a good college and then to medical school and marrying a nice lady from a better background, which of course is what I did, thereby making Mother very happy—and how the fuck come you couldn't remember this whole fucking thing?!

"What are you thinking?" Claude asked.

"Nothing," Norton replied. "When I said 'those' girls I meant the daughters of civil service . . ."

"Oh yes," Claude said.

"She was the daughter of a cop, I think . . ." Norton suddenly had to stop and swallow down a sob. It was beginning to happen again. Eileen Shanahan reminded him of Patty. Dangerous ground—he had to get off this.

"I was just annoyed with you because I felt you didn't remember what I had told you in the past about my mother's attitude toward . . ." Norton stopped again, trying to control his distraught vocal cords.

"What's the matter, Donald?" Claude asked.

"Nothing."

"There's something wrong today. I was hoping you'd get into it."

Of course it isn't unusual that Claude would notice the difference in me. This Patty thing affects my walk, my talk, everything . . . if I were my own patient I would ask what the matter is because I'm not an analyst and I would deal with my patient right up front. So why is *he* asking what the matter is? He's supposed to wait until it all comes out in associations! I'll get back to my senior year. No. He may still pursue this "What's the matter, Donald?" thing of his. No, probably not. He's probably had his one eclectic foray for the season . . . but still, back to the senior year might be construed as a dodge . . .

"I think I'm a bit disoriented over this new patient I had today."

"Oh?" Claude said, obviously interested.

"Remember last week you complained that I wasn't making any current associations?"

"If you use the word complained I get the idea that you feel I want you to give me current associations for my own needs. The analysis will go better if it's more connected to your current life, that's all."

"I suppose I took it as a derogatory remark—a criticism that I wasn't doing a proper job in my own analysis..."

"Yes, I think so. Now, I'd like very much to hear about your new patient."

"Well, I don't know why this got to me the way it did ... I've always had an aversion for people like this.... I'm glad I have this new patient so that I can get a chance to work it out ... this person is a fat, repulsive creature. I don't know if you ever had one like her, Claude, but, God, I felt like fumigating the room immediately. I almost refused to treat her. I know that sounds horrible, but that's how I felt. Well, naturally, I didn't do it. She has the unlikely name of Carmelita. She's nothing like my mother—quite the opposite, in fact ... of course, I've thought of the significance of her being exactly the opposite also ... I don't know why she affected me the way she did.... I really don't ... but all in all I believe I handled my feelings appropriately. I'll treat her, and I guarantee within three months she'll have lost forty pounds. And I'll also get to the bottom of what upsets me so much about people like that ... obviously it's something reflected in me that I haven't gotten in touch with yet—"

"Donald," Claude interrupted, "is this really what upset you?"

The image of Carmelita being caught stealing cookies from the cookie jar flashed through Norton's mind as he said, "Well, I believe so ..."

"Donald, I'd like to say something to you that you should think about."

He was stepping out of the role again.

"Yes?"

"You're editing a great deal and it has to do with something that is going on in your current life . . ."

Did Helen, his wife, call Claude? What the hell is this?

". . . now what you do is your business . . . there is no guilt or judgments here, but the blocking is getting in the way. The analysis is not going as well as it might."

No. He doesn't know anything. He's really doing his job as an analyst, it's all right.

"I-I thought it was going well," Norton said.

"It could go much better. You must say everything that comes to your mind . . . then it will go much faster."

No guilt. No judgments. He could tell Claude that he'd had an affair with a patient and Claude wouldn't come down on him with the thunderous wrath of God. The analysis. Getting in the way of the process. The process is the thing, not the events. Claude's voice was kindly and inviting. Norton loved the man—there was a warmth to his insight that Norton could feel safe with. Patty was gone for now, leaving him nothing but these rankling feelings . . . he could talk about her . . . should talk about her . . . so he wouldn't feel so bad . . . so that he could work her out and end the affair.

But as he was about to say something like . . . "There is this thing that I haven't been talking about . . ." he thought that we psychiatrists all make judgments, he knew *he* did, although he told his patients that he didn't. To Claude, Norton would be nothing but a psychiatrist who had had an affair with a patient—no matter what Claude said. Norton could work this out on his own, using the sessions to focus in on the feelings that led him into this affair and working on them without going into the goddamn thing itself—without having Claude sic the analysis on him like a vicious dog, baying to give Patty up before he was quite ready, snarling guilt-laden snarls at him . . .

Yes, he would work on working Patty out. This was the right time for it ... now that she's gone it would be easier.

"Is there anything more on this?" Claude asked.

"Well, not for the moment."

"All right, our time is up now," Claude said, rising.

Norton rose from the couch relieved that the session was over and eager to get away from Claude.

As Claude led him toward the door he said softly, "Perhaps we can go into the Eileen Shanahan association more in our next session."

"Yes," Norton agreed.

My way.

chapter three

"OH, doctor, I am taking to this therapy thing so well, am I not?" Carmelita said suddenly, interrupting her own garbled flow. She looked at him, waiting for some nod or sign of approval, but he gave her none.

"I feel a whole new life has started for me. A whole new door has opened. Oh, doctor, I must say" . . . a little hippo giggle . . . "that I think we have developed a most marvelous rapport in such a very short time, don't you?"

Norton was surprised. He said to her silently: Can't you tell I despise you? No, of course you can't. The more I despise you the more you love me. My contempt whips out at you and your skin does not welt. Somewhere underneath, you must feel my anger. If you became aware of it you would not be so fat and lonely. Who do I represent to you? Could it be your father or mother? The one that drank? Which one was that?

He looked away from her to the wall, straining to remember. With relief he remembered it was the father who drank. He who had been scoring Claude for not remembering properly had better remember things himself.

He turned to her again, continuing the silent conversation: Perhaps your father felt the same about you as I do. You have finally succeeded in getting a parent who not only never paid attention to you but was understandably disgusted by you to sit still, listen, pay attention, and act as if you did not disgust him—

Suddenly Carmelita started to move closer to him, leaning forward on her seat, slowly approaching him; her makeup breaking where her skin wrinkled; the false eyelashes unevenly put on; the flecks of dirt like huge dots in the corners of her eyes. She looked ghoulish, crazy, like a huge monster. She was going to crush him. That's it—she suddenly knew how he felt—she really heard what he was saying to her! Oh, God, had he been speaking out loud without his even knowing it?!

The sign "Freuhauff" flashed through his mind.

He had been a boy leaning against a wall and an enormous truck was backing into him; the "Freuhauff" sign on the back headed for his forehead. What did Freuhauff mean? Was it a fat German lady?—the boy Donald thought calmly as the truck was about five feet away. It will stop with plenty of space between it and me—there is no danger. Suddenly with a loud whirr of the engine the truck hurtled itself backward quickly, blurring the "Freuhauff" in the boy's eyes as it moved to crush him. The boy was paralyzed, mysteriously ready to die for some game that he did not know he was playing.

The truck driver had stopped just in time—the "Freuhauff" was an inch from his forehead. The driver had gotten out of his truck and cursed the boy.

But the boy loved that driver for having saved his life, and relished his curses.

Claude had pointed out that he might have put himself in danger in order to get a feeling of relief when he was rescued. Norton agreed—that made sense. Claude had pressed on, asking Norton how he had felt about the power of the truck and the truck driver. Did he admire it? Did he somehow want to be associated with such strength?

Norton could not connect with that.

Carmelita had stopped about a foot away from his face.

"Doctor," she said, "I am doing so well ... can I lie on the couch?"

Norton's office was arranged so that a patient could sit facing him in a perpendicular manner or could lie on the couch in the usual analytical position, in which case he would place himself behind the patient in the standard way. He preferred the sitting position for most of his patients because he felt that the facial expression was very important to a full understanding of the patient's material. However, he realized that some patients could not openly talk about very private things and face someone else at the same time, so he had the couch arrangement. And of course some people would not feel they were going to a psychiatrist at all unless they were lying on a couch.

"Yes, of course," Norton said quickly, relieved because now he would not have to look at her. He fixed the head rest hurriedly before she changed her mind.

"Oh, thank you ... thank you." She stood up, her face flushed, and looked at the couch slowly. "You mustn't take advantage of me," she said, her eyes full of girlish mischief, trying to catch his.

Norton avoided her eyes, said nothing and shifted his chair behind the couch. Carmelita took the plunge and was lying on the couch.

But she still kept her feet firmly planted on the floor.

Patty had done that when she first lay on the couch, he suddenly remembered. His mind drifted to that session... still concentrating on what Carmelita was saying, but letting pictures form in his head.

He had not wanted Patty to lie on the couch because he enjoyed looking at her. After a few sessions he had learned every nuance of movement of this doll-like, unbelievably pretty creature: the picking under her nails, the pulling of the skin on her neck, the closing of the thighs tightly together. He had played games with himself in predicting when she would close her thighs in accordance with the material she was dealing with or when she would start to pick under her nails. He began to feel that he could control her, almost like a puppet. When she would start to talk about her father, for instance, he would say to himself, Now, Patty, close your thighs as tightly as possible and pull your dress over your knees... and invariably she would. That would make him feel delighted, joyous. It was also when he would start to get those erections...

It's not that a psychiatrist is not a human being and shouldn't get an erection when looking at a pretty girl, he had reasoned. But if she is a patient then it is usually a problem. Should he refer this patient to another psychiatrist? How could he do that? What could he tell her? "I get an erection when I look at you so I will have to refer you to someone else"?

Was his sexual feeling toward her getting in the way of her therapy? Of course, normally it would, except that she seemed to be making good progress. She was talking about her problems... not nearly as much or as frankly as she should, because she was a very shy girl, but probably as much as she would with anyone. They had good rapport. He realized that she might have sensed his attraction to her, and somehow that helped her to be more free. Troubled girls like Patty get very nervous if they can't establish some sort of sexual contact with a man, and then tend to with-draw, so perhaps the sexuality of their relationship was help-ful to her ... Patty would have her sexual antennae out for any male, and if she encountered a psychiatrist who would not respond to it, eventually she might learn to deal with men on a nonsexual basis as well, but perhaps at her delicate stage she was not ready for that ... perhaps she needed this transition. Yes, he would be able to maintain this relationship with her until he felt it was time to wean her, then he would do so ...

Aren't you rationalizing pretty heavily, Donald? he had asked himself. Why not bring it up in your next session with Claude? See how it looks in the light of analysis.

Ridiculous, he had countered immediately, he knew the book on counter-transference sexuality! He knew what he was doing and he was in control of the situation. He didn't need to waste time in analysis with this kind of thing.

Then one session she had started a new set of nervous motions—a clearing of the throat he had not heard before; a crossing and uncrossing of the legs that was new. She was going to say something to him that would change their rela-tionship, and that unknown change made him wary and tense.

Finally she said in an unusually squeaky voice, "Doctor, I would like to ask you something."

He wanted to stop her. He would have liked to have frozen in time what was passing between them and to savor forever its safe deliciousness, but there was nothing he could do—no way he could stop her. He had to nod his head in assent.

"Most people lie on the couch when they see a psychiatrist and I—I think I would like to try that."

He would not be able to look at her any more! Not to see her face for the entire session was a tremendous loss to him. But if this made her more comfortable and able to relate to her feelings better, then he would have to do it.

"All right," he said, fixing the head rest slowly, waiting for her to change her mind. But she just watched him while he went through the routine, and when he was finished she took a deep breath and plunged down.

Her feet, however, were solidly planted on the floor.

She lay there for a long time in tight silence. He felt oppressed by their separation. His head was throbbing and his throat was dry. He damned the couch. He suddenly thought that perhaps she had wanted to lie on the couch to avoid looking at him because she had felt his sexuality and was running away from it. If that were so then wasn't it a healthy sign that she wanted to avoid it? No. It would be healthy if she spoke about it . . . by running away she is not dealing with it. She should talk about it. Now look what's happening. She's not saying anything. That's no good . . . what if she feels the separation from me . . . the way I feel it from her. Perhaps she didn't want to lie on the couch to get away from me . . . perhaps there was another reason . . . perhaps it was a way to get me on the couch with her?!

He tingled when he had thought that. The erection was starting again. He calmed himself and it went away. He had to assess the situation as clearly as he could.

She was still lying there not talking at all.

First step—do something.

"Why aren't you saying anything now?"

She had not replied. She was still silent, stiff, wringing her hands. Suddenly he stood up and moved his chair to the side of the couch, where he could sit facing her, looking down at her. He did it quickly before he had time to evaluate what he was doing . . . knowing that if it were a wrong move he could always retract it. She looked at him wide-eyed and surprised by the sudden move.

Then she smiled quickly and said, "Oh, yes, that's better . . ." very softly, and he smiled back quickly, and she had started to rattle on again happily in her little squeaky voice.

He felt wonderful and he was sure she did too . . . her

cheeks were flushed, her voice was bright and energetic. He had done something that was rebellious and it felt magnificent! All the psychiatrists in the world in perfect unison would have shouted that he was destructively acting out, and of course they would have been right, but here he was and here she was and she was talking and he was listening and they were both feeling just fine.

He loved the way she looked from that angle. She had put her hands under her head, which made the underpart of her breasts strikingly contoured. Her skirt was up well past her knees and she made no effort to pull it down.

His erection was there again—he didn't yell at it or feel guilty about it. He looked down quickly and was momentarily alarmed to see how noticeably it bulged. He was about to clasp his hands over it (as if in prayer) to hide it from her but restrained the motion.

If she sees it, she sees it. There's nothing horrible about it. Nothing that should really be hidden, he told himself.

So he placed his hands on the arms of his chair and listened to her. She had turned toward the wall and was talking about something that disturbed him greatly, something that made his erection go away and made him concentrate completely on what she was saying.

She had met some boy recently ... some boy who hung out in some park with a lot of other kids. It all sounded like a drug thing. This boy was nineteen years old, had never worked and was heavily on drugs. Not just a little pot, it seemed, but horse and acid and whatever else he could get his hands on. But he was so cute, she said. When she said "cute" it was almost like driving a knife into Norton. She felt that she could help him. She felt that the boy was so worthwhile, so talented, so intelligent. She didn't want him to waste his life. But she was in conflict. He wanted to go to bed with her ... she didn't know if she wanted that ... why do boys always want that?

He was upset at the type of male that silly child was becoming attracted to. He had vowed to save her from this sick relationship!

And he had! He had saved her! Who knows how she might have been dragged down by this sick boy if it hadn't been for him!

And what about now?!

She had not called him yet. She was certainly out of tranquilizers. He was still sure that she hadn't yet gone to another psychiatrist.

What a self-involved idiot he was! Here he was spending all his energy trying to work her out and he had not given one thought—not one minuscule flash of a thought to *her*. Right now she is up there in Connecticut someplace getting involved in God knows what! Confused, living away from home the first time with a new job, new living conditions, new boys wanting the same old things, and not knowing what to do. She was not in condition to go through all that along with a sudden and foolish break from therapy. She needed help.

I'll call her, he decided. I'll tell her that I'll drive up to see her once a week. I can give her a session up there. Well, of course it's unusual, but that's what's needed in this case. I'll do it. I'll call her.

He checked out how he felt after he had made the decision to call Patty and found that although he was still a bit tense and depressed he felt much better. Of course, she might reject his offer, but he would be able to see her and talk about it and who knows what might result from that. He saw a picture of himself walking hand in hand with her in a peaceful Connecticut wood. Yes, all in all, he wasn't ready to work her out yet—in time, but not yet. It would be too abrupt for her. He would call her as quickly as possible.

He even felt kindly toward Carmelita now, and if Carmelita had been facing him she would have seen a kindly, attentive smile that no doubt would have thrilled her.

He was even able to pay full attention to what she was

saying, and of all things she too was talking about a boy.

"Doctor, I must tell you ... there is this boy," she was saying. "His name is Peter. He's in my acting class. He is such a funny-looking skinny little boy with big glasses and a shaggy Buster Brown haircut. At first I thought he was weird or sick ... maybe always on drugs or something—a total washout."

"Why?"

"He sleeps all the time. He seems to be walking and sleeping at the same time. While waiting for class he sleeps and then when he gets in class he is asleep before he hits the seat. For the first two weeks he didn't get to do his scene and I noticed that he just slept off in the far corner. Then last week his scene came up. He was doing it with another girl ... they were doing a scene from *Streetcar Named Desire?* By Tennessee Williams? Have you heard of that play, doctor?"

"Yes," he replied patiently, wanting her to get on with the story, somehow very interested in hearing more about this Peter.

"Well, they were doing this scene—between Blanche and Stanley, and as they were setting up to do it I said to myself, 'Oh, will this be embarrassing.' I couldn't imagine little Peter doing the Brando role—you know, doctor, Marlon Brando the actor?"

"Yes," he replied, wondering why patients think that psychiatrists know absolutely nothing or absolutely everything.

"Well, the minute he got up there and opened his eyes he thrilled me right to the marrow. He made Brando look washed out, pale, in comparison. He was so alive, so vibrant —cruel yet kind, vicious yet loving, animal yet spiritual. His performance electrified the entire room. He was the best actor I had ever seen. When the scene was finished there was silence in the room for a second and then everyone stood up and applauded, including the teacher—and that is rarely done in acting classes. But even as they were applauding he was falling asleep and by the time he returned to his seat his eyes were closed. And not one word was said about that . . . he could do anything he wanted as long as he could perform like that . . ."

Something in Norton was stirred, gripped by this character very strongly. To be superb yet oblivious; to sleep all the time soundly, blissfully, and to awake just to tap dance on the cap of ecstasy and then go back to sleep again; not to have to deal with wives who make silly demands; not to have to listen to patients whom you really can't do very much for; to sleep through all this and then to wake up at the point of . . . where? Momentarily he blocked the point of ecstasy that he felt was the only point worth being awake and alive for, but then he let it through. To wake up at the point at which you are coming in Patty and your whole conscious and subconscious and universal unconscious and intellect, spirit, and whatever the hell else there is starts at the fermentation in your testicles and continues through your penis and is fulfilled by the flowing, flexing and spilling; and then the process is renewed by the floating to hazy, weightless sleep buoyed by her breasts . . .

Norton looked at his watch and saw that the session had gone a bit past the time.

"We'll have to stop now," he said, interrupting Carmelita.

". . . when I walked outside after class it was drizzling . . ." she went on, ignoring what he had just said.

"We have to stop now," he said more insistently, standing up imposingly in front of her. She stood up and headed toward the door, not pausing a moment in the recital of her story.

. . . "and I saw Peter, asleep on the hood of a car parked right outside the studio . . ."

"We'll continue this the next time," Norton said, holding the door open for her and ushering her out.

"The poor darling! I lifted him off the hood of the car . . ."
she was saying as he gently but firmly closed the door.

He went quickly to his desk for his address book. Patty
was renting a house in Connecticut with some other people.
He had a few minutes before he had to leave for his session
with Claude. He located her address and dialed information
and after three rings the operator answered.

"Information. What town, please?"

"Old Saybrooke."

"Yes."

"I want to call the phone at 24 Pond Road in Old Saybrooke, please."

"What name?"

"I don't know what name the phone would be listed under.
The person I am trying to reach, a patient of mine, rented
this house with some friends but I'm pretty sure the phone
is not under that person's name."

"I cannot give you a phone number unless you have a
name."

"You can look up the address and give me a phone in the
house, can't you?"

"We do not have address listings in Old Saybrooke."

"Oh, I see. All right, thanks."

He was about to hang up when he heard her say, "Perhaps
you can give me the name of your party anyway. It might
be listed."

Norton did not want to give this operator Patty's name. He
didn't like her insinuating, knowing voice. She was probably
one of those busybodies who make up stories about people
who call for information. He had already told her that he
was a doctor calling a patient. So when she heard Patty's
name she would think, Oh, this must be a young female
patient that this doctor is calling. Sounds like he really wants
to get in *touch* with her. I bet there's something going on.

He yelled at her silently, I am trying to *help* her.

He decided to give the operator the name anyway. "Her name is Patricia Hume," he said, restraining himself from adding such things as "I am her doctor and I am trying to help her."

"How do you spell that?"

"H-u-m-e," he said, regretting the whole thing, getting nervous because he was bordering on being late for his session, dreading the opportunity Claude would have to ask him why he was late.

"Thank you. She is listed at 24 Pond Road. It is a new listing. Please note the number."

He felt instantly exhilarated as he copied the number down. There it was right here in his address book—his pathway to her. And she has a phone in her own name, he thought—amazing, good sign of responsibility. She is using what I taught her.

"Thank you very much, operator," he said warmly.

"You're welcome."

He looked at his watch, noted that he would be able to make his session on time and decided to call Patty that very evening from home. . . .

In the session he felt that the essence of his involvement with Patty was locked up inside his father, something about Father that fitted in with Patty, that was triggered by hearing about Carmelita's Peter. He'd been scouting early-childhood recollections of Father when Claude asked, "What kind of relationship did you have with him?"

Relationship? The man who was Norton's father, the man with close-cropped wavy hair, tough face, in shirt sleeves reading the *Daily News*, smoking a cigarette, not looking at him or Mother, was not the sort of man that one had a relationship with.

"I didn't have one. I never remember my father talking to me directly. If he wanted me to do anything or wasn't pleased with something I was doing he would whisper to my mother, loud enough for me to hear, of course, things like, 'The kid's always got his nose in a book' or 'How come he ain't out there with the other kids?' I never remember him using my name. I was always 'kid.'"

"How did that make you feel?" Claude asked.

"Detached, very detached. I mean, I was linked to Mother but there was never any link to Father except... except he would look at me sometimes with a half smile and a knowing look as if we shared something in secret. I loved him when he did that but I didn't know what it was... but it was special.... I wish I could describe it."

"Could you put words to what you feel your father was trying to tell you?"

"Words?"

"Make up a dialogue."

"Fantasize a dialogue. That's an excellent technique, Claude."

He was silent, waiting for Claude to say "Thank you" to the compliment. Claude said nothing and Norton quickly realized that he would rather have gotten off into a discussion of the technique than do what Claude asked.

"You want me to make up a conversation between myself and my father?"

"Yes."

"I never had a conversation with my father."

"Ask him in your imagination now what he meant by those special looks ..."

"I can't even imagine asking my father anything."

Claude was silent.

Norton pictured his father in the kitchen, the same cigarette, the same paper ... mother off in a corner somewhere cleaning something. Norton could not, even in his imagination, say anything to his father but he was able to indicate with raised eyebrows and open hands that he wanted his father to speak to him.

"I can hear him saying something like, 'Listen, kid,'—he's saying this furtively so that mother can't hear. 'Listen kid, I got it made. I go to work, I don't do shit on the job, and everybody is happy because nobody expects anything but shit, see. Don't let your mother know I used such a word with you or I'll knock you on your ass.' Funny, as he's telling me this he seems to enjoy the fact that he is doing it under Mother's nose."

"Yes . . . go on . . ."

" 'Then when I come home I get everything I want without even thinking. She thinks of everything. Being taken care of like that—not having to worry—doing what the hell you want—that's what life is, kid—finding a cushy deal. Everything else is a bag of bullshit.'

"God, as I see him now his eyes are shining with a sneaky religious fervor. He has found his truth—his God."

But now Norton's father, carried away by an almost religious fanaticism, moved closer to Norton. He was going to whisper something to him that Norton did not want Claude to be privy to.

" 'And, kid, you've got to have someone on the side . . . someone who really loves you . . . worships you . . .' "

"Patty. Patty, Dad . . . I've got Patty . . ."

But Dad wasn't paying attention. He was shaking his head, reading a letter from school. Norton decided that he could let Claude back into his associations now but he felt a sharp, bitter disappointment that even in his own fantasy his father couldn't smile and look at him approvingly.

"Now wait a minute," Norton said.

"Yes?"

"He is angry at me. I fucked up. He is holding a letter from the school and shaking his head woefully and angrily . . ."

"What kind of letter?"

"One of those letters of praise that principals write . . . you know, one of those 'We are proud of your son' letters. . . . 'Jerk,' he said, 'you're showing them what you can do. If you show them that you can do then nobody does it for you! You're such a little jerk.'. . . He shakes his head and goes back to his paper, not wanting to be bothered by my existence any more."

The image of Peter asleep in a corner flashed through Norton's mind.

Yes, Norton thought, falling silent. Peter gets taken care of just like my father. The world is Peter's civil service and Carmelita is his mother and he can have as many worshipful idols as he likes because he's talented and young. Young. I'm forty now. I'm not going to get anyone like Patty after this. I've sustained myself all these years only because somehow I knew that she would come along. All those years with the dullness of Helen I knew that Patty was on the way. And now that she's here I can explore my psyche all I want but I'm not giving her up.

Passivity, Donald.

Yes, passivity . . . call it what the fuck you want but I'm not giving her up!

Patty and Passivity.

Yes, passive. Yes! Buoyed by her breasts—totally accepted . . . be nothing but yourself and be worshiped for it. A cushy deal. Yes. You're right, but I'm not giving her up!

Who was he talking to?

His own analyst. In his head. Claude was forgotten. He was Donald, the analysand, and this was Dr. Norton, the analyst.

"What are you thinking?" Claude asked.

"I went blank," he said.

There was more silence.

"Your eyes have been closed during the entire session," Claude observed.

Norton immediately opened them. He felt flustered, caught off guard.

"So? Permissible, isn't it?"

"It's the first time I've observed that. Is there any significance?"

"I don't think so."

Silence.

"You think I said that too fast, don't you?" Norton said.

Silence.

"Perhaps it was too fast. Perhaps I still have a conflict between what I considered my father's passivity, symbolized by the closing of my eyes, and my own assertiveness. . . ." He felt safe rattling these things off and he continued to do so until Claude interrupted him.

"I was hoping that you'd explore the feeling more by bringing it up to your current life."

How badly he wanted to look at his watch! How badly he wanted to get off by himself and think about Patty and Passivity! The power of Passivity! But he dared not make a move and risk Claude's picking it up as a further resistance. Perhaps he ought to issue a little bulletin on current events of the week and give it to Claude each session, thereby satisfying this insatiable desire that plagued Claude; then at least they might have a session where he could get on with his analysis the way he wanted to without this interference. He had gotten to something important about Patty and now he had to stop and give Claude some stupid current events!

"I think it has something to do with the boy that this Carmelita person described to me in today's session . . ." he said, launching into the entire Peter episode, deferring any thinking he wanted to do about Patty and Passivity until later, racing toward the end of the session, grateful it was coming soon.

"Donald," Claude said after he had heard the entire Peter story and Norton's connection of Peter to his father, "why did you come into the analysis?"

"Don't you know why?"

"No, I don't."

"I'm a psychiatrist. Understanding myself more is just another way of being better at my work . . . we went through all that."

Norton had never told Claude about the pond, and the peace and calm that he wanted to achieve . . . the pond's emanation from Claude that he wanted for himself. He had kept back this deeper reason for the analysis fearing that to do so would give Claude a strong wedge, a crowbar to force him to talk about things he didn't want to talk about. When this Patty thing is over, he resolved, I'll go into that more.

"Many psychiatrists give themselves that reason for going into analysis after they've established a practice as you have, and I think it's valid—as far as it goes. But more frequently there are deeper reasons, and usually those reasons come out in the analysis."

"My current life is not troublesome."

Claude paused before he said, "I didn't say it was."

Stupid! Why did he give that gratuitous denial about his current life! It was an admission. Was Claude some kind of fucking detective? He was tired of this probing—isn't the time up now?

"There might be deeper reasons. I'll have to think about it."

Norton dared to take a quick look down at his watch. It was two minutes past the time.

Why wasn't Claude saying anything?

Norton felt that if he said something Claude would know that he was eager for the session to end, and he didn't want Claude to know that.

But he *was* eager for the session to end.

Well, he would say it and if Claude pointed up his anxiety he would admit it and give the reason that as a psychiatrist himself he was identifying with the time problem of having another patient waiting outside, even though he knew that Claude had no other patient waiting outside, but it would be enough to get him through the session . . .

"Claude," he said, "our time is up now . . . I think."

"Ahh, yes," Claude said, glancing at his watch. "We do have to stop now."

Norton felt a bit let down at not being able to use the rationalization he had so carefully prepared.

As they were getting up, Claude said, "Donald, how's your marriage going?"

"Fine," he said quickly, pleased at his easy response.

At least, as far as I'm concerned.

chapter four

NORTON noticed that Tom the elevator man wore his white gloves.

"Got them on today, huh, Tom?" Norton commented.

"Oh," Tom said, startled at hearing the usually silent and morose doctor speak to him at all and especially in such a jaunty and friendly way. "Well, some of the people did complain, you know."

The elevator door had closed and they were traveling up.

"Snobbish absurdity," Norton said, referring to the tenants in his Central Park West cooperative who insisted that white gloves be worn by the elevator men and doormen.

Tom did not reply, but as Norton stared at the back of

Tom's neck he knew that Tom was grateful for his observation. He always knew that Tom and Frank the doorman hated this archaic sign of servitude, and he had always wanted to let them know that he sympathized with them and that he was not one of the tenants who participated in such nonsense. He felt very pleased with having expressed himself to Tom and was eager to do likewise to Frank as soon as possible.

When they came to his floor and the elevator door opened, Norton saw that the *Times* was not on his door mat.

"Did the *Times* come today?" he asked Tom.

"Yes, sir."

"Umm, I wonder where it is?"

"Oh, well, the missus probably took it in."

"The missus?" Norton said numbly. Helen must have come back to get some things. How the hell was he going to make that phone call?!

He had to escape immediately.

"Take me down again, Tom. I forgot something."

Tom was so fucking *slow*. The back of Norton's neck almost burst as Tom slowly closed the elevator door. His eyes were fixed on his apartment door in fear that at any moment Helen would open it and be there looking him in the eye, stopping his escape, wanting to deal with things. He almost told Tom to hurry but he did not want to appear peculiar.

He had a strong impulse to caution Tom about saying anything concerning his presence. But Tom wouldn't say anything anyway, would he? The only reason Tom mentioned Helen to him was because of the *New York Times*. Still, Tom is more chatty with women than he is with men (wonder if it's true that he's had affairs with some of the women in the building? Helen? Norton giggled to himself. That would be funny.)

Irrelevant associations right now, Donald. What to do? If she knows I'm about she'll sit in the apartment waiting for me, and where will I be able to make my phone call? The elevator had almost reached the ground floor and Norton almost said something like, Now, Tom, make sure you don't tell Mrs. Norton about my being here.

But then Tom would have said, But why, Dr. Norton?

And Dr. Norton would have said, Well, Tom, because that fucking woman wants to deal with things and I'm just not in the mood, that's all. She wants to talk about divorce or reconciliation, lawyers or marriage counselors. I don't want to break things up. We can go on just the way we had been going on, actually it would be better for you.

He was talking to Helen—talking to her the way he had talked to her the night Helen left the house.

The elevator reached the ground floor and he felt safer. He had a strong feeling of kinship with Tom. They were men together, weren't they? They had wives to dodge and girl friends to please, didn't they? He had a strong urge to ask Tom to come with him to the little bar on Columbus Avenue and he'd buy Tom a drink and tell him all about his sweet little Patty, and Tom, in turn, would talk about some of the women he'd made it with ... perhaps in the building ... they'd laugh it up together ... have real fun, just like the men did in that little bar around the corner from where he lived as a teen-ager. Was it Casey's or O'Brien's—he didn't remember ... all he recalled was that for some inexplicable magnetic reason he had always wanted to go into that bar. There was something dark and secret but also beautiful and fun there, and the figures that he could vaguely see through the dirty beer-advertising windows were dreamlike, vaporous but happy. Happy, slightly tipsy ghosts.

Once when he was going home at night he had to urinate urgently. This would be his opportunity, he decided, to finally get inside the bar. After all, it was an emergency and he couldn't wait to go home, he reasoned, setting up his arguments for he knew not whom. He had opened the door quickly and walked in, his eyes searching for the sign indicating the men's room, feeling lost when he didn't see it. The bartender, a man he had never seen in the neighborhood, looked at him inquiringly. Norton had quickly said, "Got to go to the john," but in the middle of saying it he saw his father at the bar. He saw his father . . . with some men, men he worked with in the Transit Authority . . . drinking beer . . . they were in the middle of a laugh . . . and they were surrounded by women . . . mostly big, blowzy women with cleavage and dyed hair except for the one his father was talking to. She was a small, dark woman, who smoked a cigarette and looked intently at him as he talked to her the way Norton had never seen him talk to Mother or to him. She was part of the bar scene but separate . . . an older woman but with a young curve in her cheek, dark hair . . . color of Patty's . . . but short in that style of the day—an intelligent, sensitive woman, sad in her eyes and just a little sexy to young Donald. And Father, Father was talking to her . . . straight on . . . right in her eyes and she in his. His entire being seemed to march with life . . . so different from the listlessly sardonic stillness of his at-home pose. His father had stopped in the middle of a quiet, unsarcastic laugh and looked questioningly at him, and Norton had said with a weightless voice, "Got to go to the john," hoping that he could also imply to his father that it was a real emergency and he wasn't interfering or anything. His father had nodded to him imperceptibly, and then miraculously the men's room sign loomed in front of him and he was inside trying to go to the bathroom. But he couldn't go. He felt guilty for being there, trapped, and wished that he could escape without going through the bar again.

He had caught his father having fun! No, more than that! He had caught his father being a man, a full complete man, because the worshipful eyes of a pretty woman is what a man needs. It could be the only thing that kept his father together . . . it's the only thing that can keep anyone in balance . . . the having it or the hope of having it—without it a man can just slip away . . .

He heard one of the men say something loud and lewd and one of the women laugh raucously, but then the laughter stopped as if someone had ordered it shut off. Norton had been uncomfortable, unable to relieve the heavy pressure of urine, imagining his father's fury at him for interfering in something important. His father would take it out on him directly now because he couldn't very well tell his mother to do it; because if he did that then his mother would know that he was drinking at a bar . . . fooling around with women . . . telling dirty jokes and stories. His father had never been directly angry with him before and he felt that the onslaught of his father's wrath would be enough to make him burst into pieces. He had fled the bar without a glance at anyone . . . fled it just as he had fled his apartment door just now . . . and the feeling was the same, he connected suddenly now, as the elevator let him off.

In both instances he felt he was doing something horribly wrong.

Bullshit!

He was lucky that he could analyze himself . . . dissect these feelings and isolate them for what they were . . . insidious microbes of guilt, trying to infect a healthy mind.

He glanced back at Tom as Tom stood by the elevator door, and smiled slightly to him. Tom smiled back. Two men of the world. Sure, he could sit at a bar and drink with Tom and indulge in that most universal symptom of neurosis known to man—namely, treating women as sex objects— but he wouldn't. He was past that. He was going to stop acting that kind of thing out at every level, just as he had stopped doing with Helen recently. He had pardoned Helen from the sex-object prison. Why couldn't she see that? Why was she carrying on so? Why was she preventing him from making this phone call from the apartment?

Frank the doorman noticed with surprise that Dr. Norton was smiling at Tom. What's gotten into that sourpuss? he thought. Will I be gettin' a little smile and a nod also from the good doctor like as if I were a human being all of a sudden? Dr. Norton walked right past Frank without a nod, and Frank watched the good doctor as he paused momentarily in front of the building and then quickly walked across the street and sat down on a park bench.

What the hell is he up to? Frank wondered. There's trouble up there, I know that. I wonder if he's trying to avoid the missus? I wonder if the missus has left him? God help the good doctor if she has. Jesus, he couldn't wipe his own ass if she didn't unwrap the toilet paper, tear it off and fold it for him. Frank looked over at Dr. Norton on the park bench across the street; slumped, slightly huddled, his head shaking ever so slightly and his mouth moving. Talking out loud to himself, Frank observed. Just think: people paid money to go to him and have him tell them how to act. There ought to be somethin' done about crazy birds like that being psychiatrists.

I'll go to a drugstore to make the call, Norton thought, why should I hang around here? It's just a phone call. But then as he was about to get up and walk toward a drugstore he pictured talking to Patty and being interrupted by an operator asking him to put money in the machine and having people stare at him in the booth, and he stopped.

He would wait a little while.

So he sat on a park bench across the street from his apartment house, wondering how it had come to pass that he was on a park bench waiting to get into his own apartment.

"Did I handle this whole situation with Helen right? he asked himself, quickly aware that he was talking out loud, stopping himself lest someone think he was weird.

He couldn't think of anything wrong that he had done.

It was her doing, her own middle-class morality, surprising in one who came from a family of old money.

Easy to say that. But how would it stand up in the light of analysis? Maybe I should have talked about this in my sessions with Claude? No, no, I don't need Claude to help me with my present life; I just need the structure of analysis to delve into my past and help me put that together. I can handle my own present. I can analyze this situation and see where it went wrong all by myself. I can connect my own past to my present and work out my own distortions. I did it before—

Then why are you in analysis if you can do that?

The idea of the pond and the peaceful but powerful image of Claude came to him.

I am close to that peace and I am close to that power. The way to it is to be totally self-contained, to be totally in command of how you feel and how you act at each moment. To be able to analyze yourself, to be able to come to your own resolutions, to be honest enough to face everything about yourself.

He leaned back on the bench, physically becoming the analysand and mentally putting himself in back of the analysand and so becoming the analyst as well.

I felt wonderful that night, Donald-analysand began.

Um huh. Dr. Norton-analyst nodded. He liked it. It would work. He continued.

I had just made love to Patty that afternoon and I felt immersed in a total pool of warmth. I had never felt that way before. I was bathing in how good life was. So help me, doctor, never before—I mean, valedictorian, medical school, having children, the whole thing in life up till the age of forty and I had never felt this beautiful and this much in command of everything. This experience with Patty released a surge of appreciation for how good life was to me. This may sound funny, but I looked at Helen when I came home and I really could appreciate what a good wife I had. She was competent and content with having achieved what she wanted to achieve in the world.

I had succeeded in rewarding her for putting me through medical school by giving her exactly what she wanted in life —a two-child family, marriage to a prestige-type person, living in a prestige-type place, enjoying a cultured, well-rounded-type life. I felt good that I gave her these things. There were two letters from the children away at camp and I felt grateful, really, for having two very nice, well-mannered boys seemingly free from neurosis. No money worries; the best of health; and next week Patty would be there again at the same time in the same place. Do you see how I felt?

Dr. Norton was silent.

Donald tensed. Would the doctor question his having this kind of relationship with a patient? Would he suggest that his euphoric mood was based on neurosis?

Yes, Dr. Norton replied. I see how you felt.

Donald went on, grateful for not being sidetracked by those other things.

I remember looking in the bedroom mirror just before we were going to bed that night, thinking whether or not I should grow a moustache. Patty liked men with moustaches. She said they looked so cute. You know, doctor, I get this strange little pang whenever she talks about someone else being cute. Don't tell me. I know it's a bit of jealousy, but I'm human. Why not? Funny, I never felt really jealous of Helen, did I? Well, anyway, I looked at the upper right hand corner of the mirror and noticed that Helen had moved to my bed. She was propping herself up on one elbow reading a book, and I realized that she was in her sex position, wearing her sex uniform. You know what I mean . . . black panties and black negligee lying on my bed to let me know that she wanted to have sex with me. Do you know what picture came into my mind? I saw a young soldier crawling under barbed-wire fences with shells bursting over his head and mud on his face. She was a draftee in a war she didn't want to fight and I had conscripted her. I had a marvelous revelation and I turned around to her. She closed the book and looked at me and said, "Thinking of growing a moustache, Donald? Really, you were never so vain before." I didn't answer, letting what I suddenly knew go through me. I think she sensed something new . . . a new power, an aloof kind of force; and her eyes were momentarily wary of it. Then she casually undid her negligee and let it fall open at the front. I knew what she was doing as I approached her. I knew she was taking soundings of her body, seeing if she were relaxed enough to have an orgasm this time. Like the soldier going into battle checking his equipment. I hovered over her, looking at her breasts and her skin, knowing that I could fondle her and have an erection and perform the surface ritual of sex and thereby keep her from the deeper experience of truth. But for the first time in my life I felt in total command of the situation. I sat down on the bed and said very gently to Helen, "Darling, I want to talk to you about something we've never really talked about before."

She said something like "Talk later" and she tried to move in on me but I took her negligee and closed it ever so deftly, and she flinched and looked at me in a way I had never seen her look at me before. I said to her, "Sex is a burden to you, Helen. I've known that ever since we've been married, and if you just allow yourself a moment to realize it right now, so have you."

She was shocked and all she could do was sputter defensively and start to talk about how she had been able to achieve orgasms lately. Very put upon as if I were accusing her of something. "I know you have and I know you've been trying, really trying, and you are to be commended for it; but, Helen, wouldn't you rather not have felt that you were forced to do the chore? Look; all ideas must be reexamined constantly. When I looked at you before propped up on the bed with this negligee on I thought of a soldier drafted to go to a war that he didn't want to fight. The old idea was that it was the highest and noblest act in the world to die in battle for one's country. We kind of laugh at that today, don't we? Now the new idea being reexamined is that everyone—every blessed mother's son and daughter of us—should *enjoy* sex to the fullest. And do you know who have been the chief proponents and pushers of this doctrine?—we psychiatrists have. For years we've been busy helping everybody achieve ecstatic orgasms. Orgasm grinders—that's what we were!"

Doctor, I was starting to feel an elan that I had never felt before. As I said it—that little pun—I said to myself that I had never been witty . . . never had a sense of humor . . . I stood up and it was as if I were addressing a large audience hanging on my every word. . . .

"But we now find that people have different sexual drives. We find that someone may have a naturally lower sex drive and be naturally content with less sex, and that this is not a sickness and this is not a neurosis. Most of the time the sickness appears due to the pressures that one feels from outside stimulis. Helen, you feel that you have to work hard and become a good soldier in a sexual war that you needn't fight. You are scratching an itch that doesn't exist."

What a good way of putting that, I've never had such a way with words before, Donald said suddenly, interrupting himself.

Yes, Dr. Norton said, that was rather good.

Feeling warmly toward his analyst now, Donald continued the narrative. "And you know what?—it is perfectly all right for it not to exist. I want to liberate you, Helen. I want you to kick your vase to pieces, break your chains and do what you want to do for a change, or, better yet, not do what you do not want to do!"

It came to me as I saw the puzzled look on Helen's face when I mentioned the vase that Helen had forgotten all about the vase symbol. I used to tell her about wanting to break that fucking piece of crockery and she had forgotten it.

Were you angry with her for forgetting? Dr. Norton asked.

No, not really. Again it came as a revelation, a piece of clarification that I wasn't really changing our relationship; I was only enunciating what was really there and eliminating the hypocritical sexual act that kept us both away from discerning the truth about how we really felt about each other. But Helen, you see, could not understand this . . .

Well, do you blame her?

Are you taking her side? Conventional morality? The faithful wife? The philandering husband?

Silence.

Excellent technique, Dr. Norton. Yes, the analytical devil's advocate. A bit of psychodrama; very eclectic. Making me face how Helen must have felt. Yes, well, of course, it works; I see how she must have felt confused and perplexed and hurt.

It could have been handled differently, couldn't it? Dr. Norton said.

No, not if I wanted to be honest. Of course, I could have deceived her and not said anything and pretended I was tired and not had sex. But if I can't have an honest relationship with her, I don't want one at all.

Silence.

You can't face anything painful without some discomfort, he thought, unless you have achieved a very high level of self-insight and are constantly practicing knowing yourself, like a concert pianist who practices eight hours a day.

A blurred picture came into his mind. He shut it out.

What was that? Dr. Norton said.

I don't know, Donald replied.

Might be important, Dr. Norton pursued.

It had been his mother's face.

Ridiculous, Donald said.

What is?

This is not a mother thing! I am not on a mother-hunting

trip with Patty nor am I on a mother-hurting trip with Helen. My subconscious is brainwashed by Freud! This is not a mother thing! I am not trying to act out unresolved mother-fucking things!

Silence.

You think I'm resisting? Afraid to explore? I just don't want to waste time going down false trails.

We have time. There's no limit on this session, Dr. Norton said.

Donald focused on the front of the apartment house carefully, making sure that Helen was not there.

I see a scene from when I was a freshman at college. There's mother's face; her polite little smile and formal social manner even when talking to her own son. "Donald, now that you're in college you should be socializing more." Sure, now that I'm in college and can meet some wealthy young lady that can do me good, you want me to socialize, is that right, Mother? Before, in the neighborhood, you wouldn't even let me go to a lousy church social, where the room would be filled with Eileen Shanahans wearing high-necked, lacy see-through blouses with ironclad brassieres and wicked crosses lying on top of the curve of their breasts. Of course I didn't say that to Mother. "You should be going out with nice young ladies from sororities. I'm not one of those mothers who wants to keep her only child tied to her apron strings."

Oh, no, not your apron strings, but you want to give the apron to another mother—one you approve of, one who'll take care of your son very nicely, right? And you know, doctor, it worked out just the way Mother wanted. She loved Helen . . . wealthy, Jewish, an old-money Long Island family. She worshiped the Jews. Father was appropriately anti-Semitic. Here I am rambling away . . . of course I'm happy too. I love Helen. A first-class woman. You know, I really don't want to hurt her. There's no one I respect more.

You're getting away from the scene with your mother wanting you to socialize more.

He became uncomfortable, squirming on the bench.

Why are you uncomfortable?

There is an advantage, I see, to having your analyst in your own head. You feel my discomfort without my telling you.

Yes.

I was so frightened of all those girls at Columbia. I was younger than most of them and I felt so much more secure with those glossy magazine pictures hidden under my mattress—where the girl's breasts were bare and free and very accessible to me and where I didn't feel like telling some eighteen-year-old girl that I was only sixteen but wanted to suck her tit anyway. But there was mother urging me on to go to this social—

He stopped.

What's the matter? Dr. Norton asked.

Connections—you want connections to the present, right? I'll give you connections, but it's still not a mother thing . . . no resistance on my part . . . I'm not afraid to explore. . . . I felt the same kind of pressure then as I did that night with Helen after I had told her about relieving her of the burden of sex and all . . .

Go on, Dr. Norton said, tensing, more interested.

Helen became very aggressive . . . wanted to know what I was doing with my sex drive. I told her not to worry about me—to absorb one new idea at a time and then we would discuss me. But you see, she wouldn't accept that; and she continued to insist on my explaining what I was going to do with my needs. Well, then I did something that I really didn't plan on doing . . . you see, I became angry . . . I could feel my spine getting cold, hard and angry at her pressing me and not letting me alone. I said to her, "Helen, listen— by insisting on an answer to that question you're taking on the responsibility of the knowledge that you will gain from the answer. I don't feel that you are able to accept that responsibility at this time."

But then she drew herself up with a great deal of dignity and said—very well, too, I thought—"Well, fine, if I am going to be free of the burden of sex, it's going to give me time to cope with deeper issues. Tell me about your new freedom, Donald."

So I told her. I told her that I did have a new sex partner but that essentially I did not want to change our relationship. Of course after that things just fell apart. She threw some things in a bag, saying that if I wouldn't leave the house, which I thought was absurd, she would. So she went to stay in her father's big house on Long Island.

Are you angry at her? Dr. Norton asked.

Furious at the ridiculous way she's been acting! If she'd only accept what I'm trying to do, she'd be happier!

You were making connections with when you were a teen-ager, Dr. Norton said, bringing Donald back to the connections.

Mother kept pressuring me to go to that social and I kept trying to get out of it. "Mother, I don't need to socialize!" I finally said, and my spine got cold with that same hard anger.

"Don't need to socialize? Why, we all need to socialize, Donald ... people need people ... young men and young women ... I can't wait to see you dating nice young ladies."

"But I don't need that, Mother."

"You don't need that? What do you mean, Donald?" She was getting worried that I might be a homosexual. She was pressing me with that dramatic I-am-pursuing-a-terrible-secret attitude that she got from soap operas on TV ... her voice heavy with emotion ... "What do you mean, Donald?"

She was insisting just like Helen was insisting, Dr. Norton said.

Yes ... yes, just like Helen was insisting; the same kind of pressure ... finally I said to her ... "Mother, I don't like boys. That's not why I don't want to go to that social ... let's forget it, huh?"

But she kept on and finally I said to her, "Mother, you see, I masturbate."

She couldn't believe that. She just stared at me wide-eyed, so I continued.

"I masturbate. I really find that much better at this stage of my life than going out and meeting these fatuous young women."

Donald laughed.

Mother was unbelievable.

Why? Dr. Norton said.

I can see her now ... I've just laid this so-called terrible thing on her, right? And the tears are welling in her eyes. You know, she's in the middle of the entire mother-hysteria syndrome and the first thing she does is ask me what "fatuous" means. And I give her the definition and she makes a mental note of it to use with her friends next Tuesday at Bingo and of course to identify the fancy word as coming from her brilliant son—all the while suspending this onrush of panic and tears. ... As soon as she fixes the definition in her mind she feels secure enough to cry and rush from the room trailing sobs behind her.

Can you see now where you went wrong? Dr. Norton asked. Can you see now why you are on a park bench waiting to get into your own apartment?

I chose a woman like my mother when I chose Helen. I chose a woman who could not accept the real me. Mother should have been able to accept the fact that at that stage of my life masturbating was better than socializing. Helen should be able to accept now that what I have with Patty is better than observing some conventional morality that is not suited for either of us.

He had come to the answer. He had worked it out. The

session was over and he was tired of waiting, so he decided to take a taxi to his office and make the call from there. He marveled as he made the decision at the wonderful way that his mind worked, noting that as soon as he had perceived the truth he was able to take constructive action. He rose from the park bench to hail a passing cab and at the instant that the taxi was pulling up to him he saw Helen emerging from their apartment house across the street with a suitcase in her hand.

Fearing that Helen would spot him, he turned around quickly and just stood there completely frozen.

The cab pulled up and waited for the man who hailed it to get in but nothing happened. The cab driver rolled down his window, leaned over and said, "You want a cab, mister?" to the man's back. The man almost imperceptibly shook his head to say no and remained stiff like one of the trees.

"Jesus," the driver said, thinking that it was weirdos like this who made the park unsafe.

Helen had seen the cab from across the street.

"Taxi!" she shouted.

Norton was stuck there. He dared not move lest Helen notice him walking away. He would stand there, right there, totally still, and she would get in the cab and not notice him.

He heard the cab door open and close on the street side. And then for some unknown idiotic reason the cab just seemed to stay there. His heightened suspended self became entwined with the rough, rhythmic idling of the engine. He strained to hear the welcome sound of the engine shifting into low and growling away, but it just idled there for what seemed like ten minutes.

"Hello, Donald," he heard Helen say behind him from the cab window. "Would you like to come upstairs and talk?"

He stopped himself from turning around to answer to his name.

She could not swear it is me. She does not see my face. If

I just stand here and not move she will go away, and in the future I will deny that this is me.

He just stood there.

"Donald," Helen said, softly, insistently, "please..."

If she gets out of the cab I will walk away. I will casually but quickly walk away and she will never be able to swear that it was me.

"Donald," she said, coming to the end of her patience, "this is ridiculous."

If she runs after me I will run away.

"You know that guy, lady?" he heard the cab driver say. "Jesus!"

There was no answer—only a very long silence. Norton tensed himself, picking out which way he would walk, listening for the sound of the cab door opening and Helen coming out after him.

But then miraculously, happily, he heard the engine shift into low and move away.

He stood immobile for a good minute before he allowed himself to look over his shoulder to make sure that the cab was gone. I handled that well, he told himself as he headed back to his apartment. Helen has to come to her own decision about me. She either has to accept this new aspect of my personality or not. It is entirely up to her. Any talking with me at this point would only confuse her.

Norton nodded and smiled to Frank the doorman as he walked past, wondering if Frank had witnessed the scene across the street. Well, if he had, Norton felt, he could only conclude that whatever had happened had been handled with force and decision on Norton's part, judging by Norton's jaunty walk and his bright smile and nod. Indeed, didn't Frank smile back at Norton with a sort of surprised delight, as if approving this new vigor of mind and body?

As Norton got on the elevator Tom said, "You just missed your missus."

Norton just grunted, wondering if Tom knew that there was trouble in Apartment 3A and concluding that he probably did, and so what. Everything was perfectly under control.

Norton let himself into his apartment, and he immediately felt like an intruder—not an intruder in place but an intruder in time. It was early evening, six-thirty, and he had not been in the apartment at six-thirty since Patty had left. As he turned the light on in the long hall he realized that the house was facing him, demanding to be lived in, asking him to move in it, sit in its chairs, turn on its radios, eat in it. He had not come here to do that, he had come just to use its phone, but the house wanted more; and Norton just stood in the long hall, unable to give it more for the moment but unable to use its phone so abruptly either.

He forced himself to walk to his bedroom where the phone was, defying the house—Helen's house, for she picked everything in it—to do anything about it, walking warily lest it spring out at him, returning his defiance with its own. As he opened his bedroom door he realized that Helen could double back and catch him in the apartment if she had a mind to do so. He walked back, easier now, and latched the front door and returned to the bedroom.

He took off his jacket and shoes, loosened his tie, sat on the bed, picked up the phone and dialed Patty's number. He did not breathe while he heard the mechanism winding its way toward Connecticut.

A young, almost hollow voice said, "Hello."

Was it she? He was afraid to assume that it was. "Hello, is Patricia . . . Patty Hume there?"

"This is Patty."

Yes, now he could tell it was she. He should have known it from the beginning. He had sounded so stiff and formal.

"Hello, Patty, how are you?"

"Is this Donald?" Patty asked.

"Yes, it is," Norton answered, straining to know if she was glad to hear from him. There was an almost imperceptible pause. Was she going to hang up? Brush him off?

"How are you, Donald?" Patty said, neutral, friendly, noncommittal.

"Oh, I'm fine. How are *you?*"

"I'm fine."

"How're you doing?"

"I started working last week. It's good . . . I like it."

"Fine."

"I'm sharing this house with about five kids who work around here. They're nice. And it's so beautiful up here, it really is . . . not like the city."

"Yes, I know it's beautiful up there. How do you *feel?*"

"Oh, all right. A few adjustments, you know . . ."

"Have you established any connections as far as therapy goes yet?"

"No, not yet."

"Oh." There was that kind of pause again that was so frightening because Norton felt that if he did not say anything she would say quickly, "Well, I have to go now. Goodbye."

"You should see the patient I've gotten to fill your time slot," Norton said.

"Oh, a woman?" Patty asked, a playful lilt in her voice.

"Would you be jealous?" Norton said, smiling.

"Well, I don't know . . . doctor."

"Well, it is a woman—and what a woman."

"Oh," Patty said, and stopped. Norton had made her jealous. He really didn't want to go that far.

"She must be all of three hundred pounds," Norton said quickly.

Patty laughed.

"By the next session I'll probably need a new couch."

"Oh, Donald," Patty laughed. "You're terrible. I can imagine what you say about me."

"How long a drive is it from New York to where you are?" Norton asked.

"About two hours."

"I was thinking maybe I could come up and visit you . . . maybe tonight or tomorrow night . . ."

"Oh, that's nice that you want to come up and visit me . . ."

"Well, I'm concerned about you . . ."

"Oh, that's very sweet, but, look, I have all kinds of things to do the rest of this week. I'll be in the city on the weekend. I have to get some clothes at home. . . . and I want to see my mother . . . she's not feeling well."

"And your father? Do you want to see him, too?"

"I don't want to think about that," she said.

"Why don't you see me when you come in this weekend?" Norton asked.

"Well, I won't be in for very long."

"Look, Patty, you should deal with this father issue, don't you think? If you don't, you know how you'll get."

There was a long pause before she said very softly, "I don't want to come to your office."

"Of course not. We'll meet somewhere. In the park . . . Central Park . . . what time are you getting in?"

"I don't know. One of my friends is driving in."

"I'll give you my home number and you can call me when you reach New York. I'll be home the whole day."

"Won't your wife mind your working on Saturday?"

"I—I don't live with my wife any more."

"Oh, I am sorry to hear that," Patty said. Norton searched her voice, hoping to hear that she was glad. Patty had always known that he was married and it had always disturbed her.

"Take down the number," Norton said. He gave her the phone number and she copied it down. Norton made her repeat the number. She did.

"By the way," he said, "I was glad to see you got a phone in your own name. That's really being adult and responsible."

"Oh, thank you."

"Now you will call me on Saturday, won't you? Whatever time you get in, right?"

"Yes."

"Promise?"

"I promise."

"Good."

It was time to say goodbye and they both felt it.

"Well, goodbye then, till Saturday . . ." Norton said.

"Yes . . . oh, Donald, I have this really great tan . . ."

"I can't wait to see . . . You know, I'm thinking of growing a moustache."

"Oh, wow," she said laughing. "All your women patients better watch out."

"Well, I'm just thinking of it."

"Goodbye, Donald."

"Goodbye, Patty."

They hung up at the same time.

He was elated. He walked up and down the room just allowing himself to puff up with a rush of well-being.

Suddenly he felt hungry. He walked to the kitchen and opened the refrigerator. He looked sadly at the half-filled jar of peanut butter, the three eggs and the fizzed-out bottle of Seven-Up that stood there to answer his need. He felt angry at Helen for not providing food. Well, he would go out to eat, although he was getting a bit bored with doing that. Since Helen had left he had been going to avant-garde movies, chamber concerts, out-of-the-way eating places and off-off-Broadway plays—things that Helen never liked to do. He had made sure that when he came home at night the only thing he needed to do was sleep. The apartment had been his bedroom and the city had been his home.

He would go out to eat again. He would celebrate in a nice little Italian restaurant that he had discovered near the house—get a little high on the wine, and then perhaps he would go to a movie—a trashy movie . . . just to see what it would be like. He smiled at the idea and went back to the bedroom to change his clothes; but suddenly he remembered that he had no money.

Helen took care of all the money. The checkbook was in her name. They had no credit cards and it was the middle of the month when no one gave him any fees.

He looked through the drawer that Helen sometimes left cash in and found it empty. He sat down on his bed wondering what he was going to do.

He became worried about money—fearing that Helen would try to put some pressure on him because she managed and controlled everything; but he put that idea out of his mind completely, knowing that Helen would not be that way . . . she was more sensible than that.

But still he was grounded for the evening. He looked toward the bedroom and pictured himself lying in his bed thinking about being with Patty. Thinking of being with her on Saturday—thinking of making love to her again . . .

He walked toward the bedroom, double checking to see if the latch was in place on the front door.

What makes you think you are going to make love to her on Saturday? Wasn't it obvious when she didn't want to come to the office that she didn't want to make love?

He walked into the bedroom taking off his shirt as he headed toward the bed.

She sounded so composed . . . and so much looser and freer. I knew there was a wonderful personality beneath that shy-little-girl stuff. Her breaking away from me the way she did was just a first step for her . . . a healthy, positive sign. She identified me with her family, but now I must make her see that I am not like her family—not like that at all. . . . And, of course, in addition there is the traditional female concern over being wanted just for her body.

He had taken off his shirt and undershirt and he sat on the bed, leaning back and getting comfortable.

I must reassure her. All right, Donald, no sex thing on Saturday. I'll take her hand and we'll walk in Central Park, he told himself, lying back on the pillow and seeing himself idyllically walking through the park hand in hand with Patty. But then as they walked they got closer and they kissed and she was pressing up against him. He had an erection as he imagined his hands at the bottom of her breasts and as he felt her body leaning against him.

He stopped.

Here I am masturbating like a teen-age boy. This is ridiculous.

He sat up, but the freshness and shadow of her image did not go away. He leaned back again not wanting to give up the pleasure of her company so easily . . . not wanting to give up the luxury of her breasts and the warmth of her skin.

He reached into his pants, feeling his erection and seeing himself unbutton her blouse at the same time—telling himself that he could afford to allow himself to fool around a little bit but that he would stop before he came. He unzipped his pants and spread the flaps, giving his hand full access to his penis.

The scene in his mind changed and he saw very sharply and vividly how Patty had looked the last time they had made love. She had come to the office in dirty old dungarees and an old plaid shirt. She wore no bra—how loose she had seemed compared to the tight little patient who had come to him all overdressed just a few short months ago. She wanted no pretense of a session then, for she had kissed him the moment the door was closed. They had gotten to the couch very quickly and she had unbuttoned her shirt and was on her knees on the couch looking at him proudly . . . proud of her breasts and proud of the effect she could have on him. He had felt then, as he did now, that such loveliness was unbelievable. He saw himself moving in on her, making sure not to let his body block her image in his mind's eye.

He suddenly realized that he was coming.

He sat up instantly before he overflowed.

He was in time.

He leaned back, forcing his hands to keep away from his raging penis, clasping them behind his head, clearing from his head the images of Patty. But as he lay there the image never quite left . . . he could formulate no new thoughts.

Why am I stopping myself? Matter of fact, it would be better. Today is Wednesday and I will see her on Saturday. If I masturbate, my sexuality will be diminished . . . and I will be able to deal more with our relationship without letting sex get in the way. My job will be to reassure her about me, make her feel safe—actually, it will be better for me and for her if I just let myself go now.

He leaned back on the bed, raised his buttocks, took off his pants and spread his legs, letting his body completely relax as he put both hands around his penis and testicles, taking a deep breath and recalling Patty on the couch as she undid the zipper on her dungarees and kicked them off.

They lay side by side and as they kissed she had, for the first time, put her hand gently on his penis. He had been excited to see how completely lost she was becoming in her own sexuality . . . profoundly moved that he was both the cause and the beneficiary of this sensual awakening. He saw her look at him, as she had looked at him that day, with total awe as if she had come to the mountain to receive the most there ever would be to receive and she was receiving it. She would never forget this in her entire life. She would never forget him!

He was starting to come again and this time he spread his legs and stroked his penis, totally immersed in, entwined with, Patty.

The phone rang.

After the first ring he tried to continue as if the phone would only ring once then stop, but it rang a second time and he sat up and looked at it, wondering if it wouldn't be better to let it ring itself away.

But suppose it was Patty ringing him from Connecticut. He sat up and picked up the phone.

It was Helen.

He was tired now. He slumped down in the bed, at the same time feeling his semen slump down into his body and the image of Patty disappear from his mind. His hand barely held the phone and his mind barely recorded what Helen was saying.

". . . two separate rooms at the Marriott Inn on Route . . . Donald, you'd better get a pencil and write this down."

"Hmm. . . ?"

"Write this down."

"Write what down?"

"What I've just been telling you about the Marriott Inn and the separate room reservations for this weekend. Oh, yes; we will drive from the motel to the camp in one car so that the children won't wonder."

"I'm busy this weekend."

"You told me you were going to go."

"Go where?"

"Now, Donald, I called you at the office this week and I told you about the children's camp . . . the parents' weekend."

"Oh, yes, of course." He remembered the call. He had been eager to see the children and glad that Helen had wanted to go with him, hoping that she would come to her senses and come back to live with him without this turmoil that she had been causing. Now of course he had to see Patty this weekend.

"I can't make it this weekend. Let's make it next weekend."

"There is only one parents' weekend and this is it, Donald."

"Oh, they'll make an exception. We'll go next weekend."

"They will not. They are very strict. We must go this weekend."

"Helen, it's absolutely out of the question that I go this

weekend. Now you call up those people at the camp and tell them that I'm a doctor and that some sort of emergency came up and they'll let us come next weekend. You'll see . . . try it. Let me know what happens, will you? Make sure you call the children and let them know that we'll be there next weekend. We mustn't disappoint them. Oh, yes, another thing . . . Helen, you haven't left me any money. When did you plan on being around here? Or can you telegraph a check or something?"

There was a sort of gasp and a long pause at the other end of the phone as he waited for an answer, then the phone was dead. He looked at it a moment as if he could see where the voice went. He talked into it a few times until he realized that Helen must have hung up on him.

He put the phone down on the receiver.

She's never done that before. She must really be pissed. He found himself delighted.

I am not afraid to do what I want to do any more! I am not afraid of people being angry or upset with my actions! I do what I know to be right, and it is right even though it doesn't fit my wife's carefully designed plans for living! I am a free man!

I'll go to the bank first thing tomorrow morning and borrow money till the end of the month! I'll get one of those two-hour loans or something!

I don't need any money from Helen! I earn a lot of money in my own right! The bank will lend me any amount I want!

He went to the kitchen to fix himself a peanut-butter-on-a-cookie concoction, marveling at the way the mind worked in finding solutions to difficult problems once old fears had been mastered.

As he spread the peanut butter onto the cookie he thought that perhaps it was time he started to think in terms of terminating his analysis with Claude. He was handling things so well on his own.

chapter five

NORTON was cheerfully looking forward to his session with Carmelita, but he did not know why until a second before he opened the door to let her in.

He was immensely interested in this character named Peter. It was like reading a boring novel that you must read for school and suddenly in Chapter 3 finding a brilliant, fascinating personality who immediately catches you up. He was hoping that Carmelita would pick up just where she had left off and fill him in on what was happening with Peter.

As she walked in she made a surprisingly graceful pirouette. "See anything different about me, doctor?" she said. "I've lost weight. I am dieting. I've lost eight pounds since I started treatment."

There was a slight weight loss, he noted, but she still didn't clean herself or her clothing, and her makeup hung on her like caked mud on a car fender.

He just nodded his head in some sort of recognition that she had indeed lost weight, and Carmelita thereupon twirled herself onto the couch, launching into the subject of dieting.

He took his seat, breathing deeply, fortifying himself for a dull session and becoming aware that he was more than casually disappointed at her not continuing her story about Peter. He was thankful that he was in touch with his feelings so that he would not let this irrational anger (for it was irrational; a patient is not there to satisfy a psychiatrist's curiosity) upset his concentration.

Oh, God, but he could do a session like this in his sleep. He would ask Carmelita questions designed to get her to go beneath the surface of her overeating. What did overeating do for her? When did she break her resolutions not to overeat? Nowhere . . . getting nowhere; she glided away from the questions like a skater away from holes in a frozen pond.

His mind began to drift.

He suddenly wished so much that Patty were there.

He could almost feel her presence on the couch . . . ghostlike . . . sensually haunting . . .

He became aware that he had an erection.

He slowly put his hand in his pocket and touched himself to make sure that he wasn't merely imagining it—without once taking his eyes off the back of Carmelita's head, fearful that she would suddenly turn and catch him touching himself. He could feel the feel of Patty streaming through his system. His unspilled semen from the other night became alarmingly active at the slightest touch.

He took his hand out of his pocket and concentrated on a spot on Carmelita's head where her hair parted and the black roots met the pale pink skin of her scalp. He listened carefully to her descriptions of her precautions against overeating. "The trick is all in the shopping," she was saying.

"You see, I don't buy any beer or sweets or cakes, so there is nothing fattening in the house. I only have to exercise my will power once that way."

"Yes," he said more affirmatively than usual—tangible, out-loud proof that he was concentrating on the material. Encouraged by the resounding "Yes," she went on enthusiastically, minutely describing every meal.

Norton became fascinated by his ability to become absorbed in what Carmelita was saying and enjoy the sense of Patty at the same time. He wasn't sure whether he still had an erection. He reached down and put his right hand in his pocket and touched the side of his penis, feeling it three-quarters hard and very sensitive. He automatically pressed his legs together, bringing his penis, warmly cradled between his legs, in touch with his hand.

His semen almost started the journey through his penis, and he immediately drew his hand away and spread his legs.

"When you stopped yourself from buying sweets and fattening foods at the supermarket," he suddenly interjected, "did it bring up any feelings?"

"Feelings?"

"Did it remind you of anything? Anything at all?"

She was silent for a moment, putting her finger to her chin, and then with a sudden shout of revelation went off on an early experience when her mother had demanded that she lose weight. Norton listened easily.

I can think of Patty if I want to and still listen totally to this patient, he thought, I just have to keep it non-sensual, that's all . . . and I just have to not touch anything. He let himself see Patty on the couch just looking up at him, lying there silently as she had for so many sessions, hardly saying a word . . . just holding her eyes in his. He let himself think of the day . . . the first day that he had moved onto the couch with her. The day that he was in the middle of his wrestlings with his conscience about her being a patient and about Helen.

He let himself think of how all his doubts were resolved when she almost imperceptibly moved her body closer to the wall, leaving enough space for him to sit on the couch with her.

He had tingled with fearful excitement when she had done that. Was she really signaling for him to get on the couch with her? Dare he do it? He was still afraid to take a chance, but he knew that if he had a more positive indication he would do it and worry about the ethics later.

Patty had, after a few more silent moments, put both her feet on the couch.

That was it.

He had stood up slowly, ever so slowly, giving himself a chance to change his course if she objected. Her eyes had welcomed him as he sat down next to her. Then they had just remained motionless in their new position, staring at each other.

Patty had reached up and touched his upper lip slightly. "You should grow a moustache," she had said softly. He had touched her upper lip in a small imitation of her gesture. She had stayed his finger and kissed the tip of it softly. He bent down and kissed her and at once he was lying with her on the couch, finding it unbelievable that someone so pretty could kiss him the way she was kissing him, with almost deep reverence, as if she should be eternally grateful to receive his caresses and not he to receive hers. Oh, there is nothing that compares to a young girl's body! No depth, no insight, no religion that compared to the feel of the small of her back as his hand moved down under her dress, slipping easily through the elastic of her panties and sliding further down. Then he had felt a wild, unreasonable onrush that had caught him completely by surprise. He was coming, and he tried to close the doors of his penis before it all got away from him; but his efforts were like a paper barricade against a surging flood, and he came and came with compulsive muscle jerks that were uncontrollable. He had tried to hide the terrible orgasm from Patty by pulling his body away from her slightly and taking his hand from under her dress, but she had sensed his hunger without really knowing what it was and had sat up, moved to the other end of the couch, and had started to cry quietly.

After a few empty drained moments he said to her, "Patty, if you want to go to another psychiatrist I'll recommend one to you."

She had just sat there wiping her tears and controlling her sobbing.

"I'm sorry, Patty, I really am. I should have recommended you to someone else when I saw how attracted I was to you. But I thought it would pass. I didn't know it would grow. . . ."

She stood up and straightened her dress and assembled herself quietly and slowly. Norton dared not move, embarrassed by the stickiness in his pants, fearing that there was telltale moisture showing through.

"I'll recommend you to someone else . . . an older man, or a woman, perhaps . . ."

He had thought to go to his desk and give her names of other psychiatrists, but there was that embarrassment.

"Call me and I'll have some people for you to choose from . . ."

She had not said a thing. She had just looked at him with something akin to quiet amazement as he ran on like that, then she had turned and left the office.

Norton touched himself now. He was completely soft . . . safe.

". . . Mother always wanted me to be dainty and feminine and was always talking to me about losing weight . . . but she always bought loads of cake and sweets and stuff . . . Do you think there is anything to that, doctor?" Carmelita was saying.

"What do you think?" he said.

"Well, sometimes I think she liked to see me overweight . . . sort of reduced her competition . . ."

He wondered if she recognized her own pun.

"Perhaps you were responding to her unconscious wishes by eating a great deal and becoming overweight . . ."

"What does that mean?"

"Well, if your mother really wanted you to be overweight, in spite of what she kept saying, then you would pick up on that feeling and try to obey it . . ."

"Oh . . ."

"Sometimes we do what we feel someone else wants us to do—not necessarily what we really want to do ourselves . . . especially if that someone is a mother."

She was silent.

"You are trying to lose weight now—and that is good. Is there any special reason . . . or any special person you are trying to do it for?"

He would hear about Peter now.

"Any special reason?" she repeated.

"Or person?"

There was a long silence before she said, "No . . . nothing special . . . I've done that from time to time . . . you know, gone and suddenly lost a lot of weight—it's just that one day I wake up and look at myself and that's it. I go out and I diet like there's no tomorrow."

He felt frustrated with her as she went off into a long, time-consuming description, not unlike what she had just gone through, of how she had lost weight the last time she had dieted. It became apparent to him that she was not going to associate to Peter, or even to himself as the prime present cause of her losing weight. The feeling of Patty came on him again.

His penis felt warm and delicious, even through the cloth of his pocket.

He listened to Carmelita, annoyed at her as she went on

—off the point—not dealing with her central problem, even when he pointed it out to her! Just babbling along as if what he said had no meaning, and as he felt his anger more he rubbed the side of his penis, squished his legs close together and let his mind go back to the next time Patty came to the office.

Dare he? Dare he let himself go so far—in the middle of a session?

What difference would it make to Carmelita, rambling on and not listening to him? And he had to get rid of this sexuality now before he saw Patty tomorrow. If he didn't do it now he might not be in the mood later, and he would lurch at Patty tomorrow and ruin everything!

He let his mind see Patty at her next session as she had closed the door and just stood there looking at him. He had walked to her and stood before her, and she had said very softly, "I don't want to see another psychiatrist." They had kissed standing up and he had not pressed too close to her—not let himself get too excited. He had locked the office door, not because he was afraid anyone would walk in but because he knew that she would be apprehensive. He had fully closed the venetian blinds, knowing that she would want the light in the room down to a minimum because she would be shy about him seeing her body. She had gone to a corner of the office and taken off her dress with her back toward him; then she had quickly gone to the couch, still in her bra and panties. He had taken off all his clothes except his shorts and had joined her on the couch. They lay side by side, hardly touching, her hands crossed over the cleavage of her breasts and her legs slightly crossed at the ankles. As he had looked at her he had thought how tight she was—how ashamed she really was of her own sexuality. He had to control himself—control his own raging sex so that she would become more comfortable, more sure of herself, not so tight. He had started to kiss her very gently, and she had warmed up. Her little arms had fallen away from guarding her breasts ... Norton was stroking himself more fervently now as he saw the sides of her breasts exposed and the bra drop away from her shoulders. God, he thought even now as he did then, her breasts are so large and magnificent for such a little girl. They had shone and glowed like wondrous magical globes, and the exquisiteness of first touching them seemed to put him in touch with the grandest mysteries of life.

He was coming now, with the vision of Patty's miraculous breasts in his mouth, while Carmelita, having discarded any idea that she went on diets to please someone she wanted to have a relationship with, was thoughtfully describing how the satisfaction of losing eight pounds made up for the pain of not eating and drinking what she wanted. The semen came out of him in a great quantity, as if it had been stored up since the last time he had been with Patty—as if the deposit had grown by compound interest, a geometrical progression. His eyes almost disappeared through the top of his head; he felt as though he were being emptied; he could feel the color draining from his face; and he suspended his breath entirely lest panting give him away.

Carmelita suddenly stopped herself, and her silence just as suddenly brought his attention back to her. He was fearful that she might have heard something or sensed something.

"Remember that boy I talked about at the last session, doctor?"

He gave her a psychiatrist's silence while he allowed himself to breathe normally and relax more easily in his seat.

"You *do* remember, do you not, doctor?"

Still afraid to talk because he might be out of breath, he said nothing.

"Why don't you answer me?"

He would, on this occasion, borrow the classical analytical technique of not replying to questions that the patients should know the answer to themselves. So he remained silent, still feeling somewhat weak and out of breath.

"There must be some special reason that you don't answer a simple question—are you awake?" She suddenly turned around and quickly looked at him, then turned back, satisfied that he was awake.

"You are awake. Then the reason you are not answering must be part of the way you treat patients, is that right?"

He felt safe enough to talk now.

"Yes," he said quickly . . . voice all right.

"I asked you if you remembered the boy I talked about in the last session? Is that right? . . . There I go, asking you a question that I don't have to ask. Is that what I'm doing, doctor? Oh, there I go, asking you a question again. A question that I should know the answer to myself. Is that right, doctor?"

"Is what right?"

"Should I know the answer to these questions that I'm asking you myself?"

"Well, let's take them one at a time."

"All right."

"Let's take the first question, which was whether or not I remembered the boy you spoke about in the last session, correct?"

"Yes."

"You wanted to know if I remembered Peter from your acting class whom you had spoken about in great detail just a short while ago, is that right?"

"You did remember!"

"Why should that be so surprising? A psychiatrist is trained to remember things."

"I must feel that I am not good enough to be listened to!" she proclaimed. "I must feel that what I say will be forgotten by the person who is listening because I don't feel good about myself! Is that it, doctor?"

74

Silence.

"That is it! I don't feel good about myself! I am always doing that to people—I am always asking them questions like that."

"Now, the next question you asked me was if my not answering you was part of the treatment."

"That wasn't the next question, doctor. The next question was 'Are you awake?'"

"It really wasn't a question, because you did something to determine whether or not I was awake by investigating for yourself. You asked a question but you were not dependent for an answer—you supplied your own answer."

"That was good, wasn't it?"

Silence.

"Oh, God, there I go again. It's a habit, isn't it? . . . Oh, *God*, there I go again." She laughed, and so did he.

"The next question, the one about my not answering being part of the treatment, was a legitimate one."

"It was?"

"Yes, and I answered it. As a new patient, you might not know that a psychiatrist doesn't always answer questions that are put to him, in order to help the patient explore his feelings more."

"Oh."

"And the last question you asked me before we started to unravel this was if I remembered what you had asked me just the moment before."

"Oh, God," she said, and she started to cry a bit.

"What's the matter?" he said.

"I—I feel so embarrassed."

"Embarrassed?"

"I must seem so stupid to you."

"No, it's not stupidity. It's other things, but not stupidity."

He felt close to Carmelita . . . her embarrassment connected to his embarrassment over what he had just done; her feelings of stupidity connected to his feelings of babyishness. His wet middle was the question and the drying diaper the comforting answer. Her questioning was the seeking lips and his answering was the giving nipple. Drying diaper. Yes— yes, get rid of these wet shorts and buy new ones in that men's shop on the corner—ask to go to the men's room and change them, then throw them away.

Carmelita was wiping her tears with the tissues he provided for his patients. Everything was connected.

"Now, tell me about Peter," he said, the voice springing out, pulling him away from this dangerous closeness.

"Oh, he is such a wonderful boy," she said. "He is like the world's baby. There is not anyone who knows him who doesn't love him and take care of him and worry about him. When I picked him up asleep from the hood of the car the last time—remember? Oh, there I go again. I must learn to stop that."

"Yes," Norton agreed. "Does Peter take drugs?"

"That's what I thought, so I asked him that night when I took him home with me and he told me that he didn't take a thing."

"He might have narcolepsy."

"What's that?"

"A sort of sleeping sickness."

"Oh, no; he told me that he had been checked out and that he wasn't sick or anything. He just liked to sleep and he thanked me so sweetly for picking him up off that car hood before it really started to pour; but he assured me that he would have gotten himself up in time if I hadn't come along. He also said he was glad I came along anyway."

"How does he live? Does he work?"

"That's exactly what I wondered. And, do you know, just at the moment I was wondering it Peter knew I was wondering it. He smiled at me through his almost closed eyes—he has such an adorable smile—well, anyway, he told me that he stays from friend to friend. He doesn't eat much and he doesn't take up much space and everyone likes to have him. He's like a good-luck charm. Whenever he stays with a friend they get a good part or a story published or something good like that. They fight to have him. Isn't that marvelous?"

Norton was silent.

"Oh, he has such a sweet personality. He is so magnetic and so talented. But, oh, doctor, it's such a pity."

"Pity?"

"He wastes his personality and his great talent. He doesn't put his magnetism to use. He doesn't use his potential."

Somehow what she was saying was getting Norton angry. He felt his spine start to harden with anger as she went on.

"Oh, doctor, if I could save one person like that, if I could help someone to achieve his potential to whatever extent humanly possible, then I would count myself a fulfilled person in my own right. Isn't that healthy, doctor? To want to help someone else? Isn't that healthy?"

He stopped himself from answering—this surge of anger threatened to be uncontrollable if it came out. He knew that he was overreacting ... Mother always talked that way ... a real shining candle in a dark world was Mother ...

"I talked to him about you."

"About me?"

"I know this is only my third session with you but I know you are going to do me a world of good. I know you are a marvelous psychiatrist—you've done me so much good already ... I've lost weight, I met Peter, I feel so good about myself, so hopeful. I was talking to Peter about you, talking to him about seeing you."

Worse and worse. He didn't want to see Peter.

"What did he say?"

"Well, he kept falling asleep every time I mentioned it."

Good man!

"But last night he said he would think about it."

Nagging bitch!

"If Peter decides that he wants to go into therapy I'll be happy to recommend another psychiatrist. I won't be able to see him." He said the speech carefully.

"Why?" she said in a shocked voice, raising herself on one elbow and turning to look at him. He returned her stare evenly, feeling totally assured in what he was saying.

"You see, I don't treat couples: a husband and a wife, or a boy friend and a girl friend, that kind of thing. Many psychiatrists feel the way I do and some do not. There are different schools of thought. I feel that the sibling complications that arise from this kind of relationship tend to be time-wasting and unproductive."

"But we're not a couple."

"Well, I thought . . ." he left the sentence unfinished as she shook her head in denial.

"You're living together, aren't you?" Norton said, beginning to feel uncomfortable.

"Well . . . no . . . he's staying with me for now, but he could be staying with someone else tomorrow. Peter and I are just friends. I mean, I was recommended to you by a friend and you accepted me, didn't you?"

"You're asking questions again that you know the answer to."

She paid no attention to what he had just said. She sat up and moved her face toward him.

"You did accept me, didn't you?" she said.

"Yes," he answered, "I did."

"Well, then?"

"How will he pay for the sessions? He doesn't work."

"I'll lend him the money."

"All right," he told Carmelita, "as soon as I have some time available I'll let you know. Right now I'm completely filled."

"He can use my time," she said enthusiastically. "We can alternate sessions. One session for me and one for him!"

He glanced at his watch.

"Our time is up now."

"Well, but what do you think? Will it be all right? One session for me and one for him?"

"We'll go into it more in our next session. Our time is really up now."

"All right," she said. "We'll go into it and it will be all right by our next session."

The usual procedure after a session was that he stood up and escorted his patients to the door. But he dared not stand up now in front of Carmelita, not quite knowing what his pants might reveal.

"Oh, doctor," she said, still sitting there. "This has been such a wonderful session. How am I doing as a patient? Would you say that I'm an interesting subject?"

He did not answer but instead he took out his appointment book and ran through some pages as if he were preoccupied with something in it. She had given up on an answer but was waiting for him to rise and escort her to the door as he had done the other times, glad for the moment that he was not doing so because it gave her extra time in her warm sanctuary—time that she was not paying for, a stolen thrill, like eating things she shouldn't. He vowed to change the stupid procedure of escorting patients as if he were an usher in a movie house. It was some silly overcompensation. He looked up as if surprised that she was still there.

"You really must go now," he said, desperate.

"Oh?" Carmelita said confusedly and started to rise. But before she got up she looked at him and said, "Are you all right, doctor?"

"Yes."

"You usually get up and escort me to the door."

"That will not be done any more."

"Why?"

"I think it would be better if you talked about that in your next session."

"I should talk about why *you* don't want to escort me to the door?"

"Yes. You might talk about how you feel about my not escorting you any more. It might prove quite valuable."

"I'd rather you escort me so that I could talk about Peter."

"Our time is up now."

"Oh"—Carmelita rose—"very well." She went slowly, hesitatingly, to the door, as if she really weren't sure where it was without him. "Are you sure you're all right?"

Norton did not answer as Carmelita, taking one last worried look, opened the door and disappeared.

"When did you become annoyed about what Carmelita was saying?" Claude asked.

"Just when she was talking about helping Peter fulfill his potential and all that. I didn't want her to push him. I wanted her to leave him alone."

"Why?"

Norton felt free to explore this. No direct hookup with Patty or Helen here, but of course the connection was really very strong. If he could work out this desire to be passive like Peter he could see Patty tomorrow and handle it better. The Power of Passivity would not push him into poses and attitudes that might drive her away.

He could feel Claude's interest—yes, even excitement—as he had been talking about Peter and Carmelita, and this fed his desire to go further and further.

"I know it sounds crazy. I know that anyone like Peter—like the way Carmelita describes Peter—has to be extremely neurotic and very unhappy. I know this, Claude. You know I know this, right? Oh, God, I'm asking questions like she does. Anyway, that's beside the point, isn't it? For a brief moment I had gotten caught up in Peter's personality as if I had discovered the perfect man; as if I had discovered someone who could be happy without hurting anyone, who could be loved by his friends and taken care of, who could be magnificent in his art and who could do all these things while being totally passive. For the briefest moment, mind you, it was only for a brief moment—I wanted him to bathe in his warm, happy passivity and I wanted her to just leave him alone! For every Garden of Eden there has to be a snake!"

"Does that remind you of anything?"

Norton let himself see a picture of his mother and father at the kitchen table when he was about five or six years old. He was going to talk about it freely now, not as he had done in the past by clouding his associations with jargon and generalizations. This session was real analysis, the real classical Freudian shit that they all loved to make fun of these days (including himself). It was exciting; he wanted to stop and apologize to Claude for wasting time all these months, but he didn't want to lose the momentum.

"I see this scene with my father and mother at the kitchen table. I must have been no more than five or six and already proving to be the boy genius. They were having their quiet argument."

"Their quiet argument?"

"Well, according to Mother, they never argued and were the perfect married couple. Any disagreements they had, she would always tell her friends, were settled through compromise or discussion. 'If nations were like us there would be no wars,' and she would turn to him and ask, 'Isn't that right?' Oh, she tried to pretend she was so happy."

"Wasn't your mother happy?"

"Just before Mother died she told me that if Father hadn't insisted that she stay home from work after they got married she could have been ... and I can see her eyes gleaming as she told me this ... 'an executive secretary for one of the big vice-presidents at Shell Oil ...' She always wanted to be an accomplisher out in the big world, and if she couldn't because she imprisoned herself, then she'd urge her husband, and if her husband would have none of it, then there was her son. She resented the role she made herself play, but even to the end she insisted she was happy. But Father knew it wasn't true. I can see him as she talked her 'happy talk,' his shoulder blades would tense a certain way and I could almost hear a voice coming from between them saying, 'I wish you'd cut that shit out.'

"Well, anyway, their quiet argument always had to do with some test that my mother wanted my father to take. She was forever after him to take these tests and she would always have this newspaper in her hand, the Civil Service *Leader*. It seemed that the Civil Service *Leader* was as much a part of my childhood as the old English racer in the garage or the basketball hoop on the tree. She chased him with it from year to year, from room to room; whenever I saw it in her hand there was tension and trouble in the house. And this one time it was very frightening to me because they were sitting at the kitchen table—she trying to show him something about a test that she wanted him to take and he turning away and saying nothing and looking up at the ceiling. When I walked in he stopped looking at the ceiling and he looked directly at me. Father never looked directly at me; he just never did. I stood there paralyzed with fright. 'Let *him* take the God damn test!' he shouted, and he just glared at me; and right there and then if I could have destroyed all those high marks and teacher notes that were coming from school I would have. But then my mother became furious, and somehow this scared me even more. I had never seen her get really mad. She glared at him and whispered vehemently. 'He could. And *he* would probably pass it, too.' "

Norton stopped. Mother was passive too. Her pushiness, he decided, came out of frustration over her own passivity.

He'd never thought of Mother as being passive before. He wanted to savor this, dig more deeply into it, but by himself —there were important hookups to Patty here. He stopped and wanted to look at his watch.

"What are you thinking?"

"Nothing." I wish the session would end.

More silence.

It might be interesting to tell Claude about this feeling that I want the session to end, he thought. We can play with it for a while until the session ends.

"I feel like looking at my watch to see if the session will be over soon. Resistance, isn't it?" Norton asked.

No answer.

"Silly question, wasn't it? As a psychiatrist I should know resistance when I meet it, even when it's my own."

"You're not here as a psychiatrist. You're here as a patient."

Why had Claude made that distinction? He had not gone into analysis for emotional problems. Claude knew that. Analysis was an extension of himself as a psychiatrist. They were two colleagues; and he instantly resented the typical analyst-superiority attitude that Claude had over him as a mere unanalyzed psychiatrist. But of course he wasn't going to go into all that. These were old arguments, and analysts regarded them only as forms of resistance. Their resistance was to get lost in yours.

Claude was continuing, "It's difficult for a patient at the early stages of analysis to detect and recognize his own forms of resistance. I feel that your wanting the session to be over at that point probably was resistance, but we will be aware of that feeling from now on and we will see how it operates."

"Yes," Norton said.

He still had not looked at his watch. He would try to look at his watch without Claude's noticing. As he lay on the couch with his eyes focused on the ceiling, he tried to think of a suitable subject to talk about while accomplishing this maneuver.

"I feel excellent about this session so far," he said, looking down at the hands lying folded on his lap. He could not quite make out the time without moving his head or bringing his watch closer to his eyes, and he wanted to do neither lest Claude see him.

"I took something that was currently happening, something about which I had an irrational feeling, and I hooked it into something from the past. Perhaps my problem is that I don't have too many irrational feelings and hardly any dreams. I haven't remembered a dream since I've come into analysis; of course, I know that could be a very deep form of resistance . . ."

"Yes," Claude replied, "but I still haven't heard why you are so troubled with pa—"

Was he going to say Patty?! Norton became instantly frightened, until he clearly heard Claude follow through with "passivity." . . . "why you are so troubled with passivity." Not Patty. . . . Oh God, did I get scared. I thought he knew. He calmed himself. Perhaps he could scratch his nose and sneak a quick glance at his watch.

"I wish I could remember my dreams, the answer might be there. Have you read about those recent experiments involving dream recalls?"

He launched into a rambling dissertation, being careful to generally relate his discussion to the fact that he hadn't recalled any dreams since starting analysis, but in essence keeping the subject far from himself. As he went on he found himself becoming very tense, as if he were running after robbing someone, afraid to look back yet feeling the hand of the law at his shoulder. He seemed to just go on in perpetual motion now, not even worrying about his watch, just rambling on and on. Suddenly he stopped and said, "Why are you letting me go on like this?"

"What do you mean?"

"I'm not really saying anything now. I'm off the point, totally general, acting out my resistance. Why didn't you stop me?"

"Why should I stop you?"

"Do you think it's right to let someone babble on like that?"

"I think it's better to learn to stop your own acting out rather than relying on someone else to stop you."

"What if some people can't stop themselves? What if, even if some people know everything possible about their illness, they still can't stop themselves? What then, Claude? What then?"

Claude's answer had become vital to Norton. He hadn't known that the question was in him until it had sprung out of him. But once out there it hung like an unlit light bulb waiting for Claude to reach up and pull the string.

Claude paused before he said, "Donald, you've got to force yourself to talk about what you're involved in, in the analysis. You must talk about your life now."

That has nothing to do with the question I asked you, goddammit, Norton replied silently.

And as if Claude heard the reply he continued, "The question you ask implies that there's some magic way to stop the unconscious forces in us ... doctors know a great deal about heart disease but they die of it frequently, psychiatrists have the highest suicide rate of any occupation. You must talk about your problems like anyone else, Donald ... if you're acting out, if you're making big changes in your life without bringing it into the analysis, no amount of knowledge can help you. Donald, what's going on?"

Acting out. Patty is a giant act-out. Splitting up with Helen without even bringing that into the analysis. All one huge giant act-out. Stop seeing Patty. Talk about it. Work it out. But the pictures of a fat, grinning, horrendous Carmelita blotting out Patty floated quickly through his mind. Give up Patty and life becomes Carmelita.

"I'm going to have to try the technique of waking myself up at certain intervals in the middle of the night . . . perhaps I can use self-hypnosis . . . and jotting down dreams," Norton told Claude. "I think it's all there in the dreams, Claude."

There was a long pause, as if Claude were trying to think of something persuasive to say but couldn't. Finally he said, an unmistakable note of tiredness in his voice, "Our time is up now."

chapter six

NORTON went through the entire day Saturday with the phone attached to him like another hand. He woke in the morning and went to the bathroom leaving the door open and the phone extended as far as it could go right outside the bathroom door, as though to lose the sight of it would be to lose the sound of it. He took a bath rather than his usual shower so that he could watch and hear it without any danger of running water obliterating the sound and soap in the eyes closing out the sight. When he moved into the kitchen to have breakfast he had to rely on the wall phone; but he did not want her to call while he was there because the kitchen faintly reminded him of Helen. He would feel awkward talking there. No, he wanted to talk to her while sitting on his bed, and so he rushed his breakfast a bit—finally taking his coffee into the bedroom.

From the window he could see an overcast summer day— not too much sun, not too hot. The kind of day when breezes become very important in Central Park.

A beautiful day for a walk in the park with a pretty girl.

With extreme good humor he prepared himself for a long wait, enjoying the luxury of possibly many hours to kill without anyone to divert him. He might clean up a bit, he thought, looking about the disordered, dusty apartment which had not been cleaned for two weeks. No—the thought of the vacuum cleaner running and drowning out the ring of the phone made him decide against it; besides, he had money now (his bank loan had gone through) so he could call an agency next week and get someone over to clean the place.

He settled down in front of the television and for hours became transfixed by a succession of old movies and new commercials. He didn't know when the little idea started to form in his brain that Patty might not call at all—perhaps it was always there, but by late afternoon, in the middle of his third movie, he became aware that he was very apprehensive and depressed. The day was almost gone and there would be no walking in Central Park any more if she didn't call soon. He looked out the window at people in the park, idly scanning the assortment of elderly people, strange people, ordinary people, young couples. There was one young couple against a tree, and the girl reminded him of Patty because of her long black hair. The boy was like a demonic sex freak, jamming himself into her, his kinky Afro hair making him seem like a ravenous insect. He watched them for a while, feeling that he was like that boy, a ravenous sex insect wanting to suck every bit of nectar from the lovely helpless plant. The insect crawls away; the plant is left lifeless and drained; the insect doesn't give a shit.

That isn't you, Donald, you care, you are a caring, loving

person. You care about her, you know you do. Here you are, putting yourself down, making yourself feel as if you were some sort of insect. Oh, Donald, you don't know your own good qualities. Call her in Connecticut—now—something might have happened to prevent her from coming into the city. She might be having difficulty—call her and see if you can help.

He quickly picked up the phone and dialed the Connecticut number. As he heard the phone ring he anticipated that Patty would be angry that he hadn't called earlier, hadn't worried about her when she had not called him.

Damn his selfishness!

No one answered the phone.

Perhaps at this very moment she was trying to reach him from someplace else and getting a busy signal.

He slammed the phone down.

He crouched over it waiting for it to spring into life . . . seeing her go through the paces of dialing the number again (she wouldn't give up with just one try, would she?).

When nothing happened it came to him that it really might be over.

Perhaps she just did not want to see him any more. It would be a good thing. He would talk about the entire matter in his sessions with Claude. He would call Helen and tell her to come back. The entire thing was inappropriate. His age. His being her psychiatrist. Being married. The whole thing. He should feel very happy that she was not calling.

He sat there a while, tuning in to how he felt about these conclusions, encouraged that no overwhelming depression was attacking him. He went to the window and looked outside into the park. It was getting dark now; the insect-and-plant couple were not there any longer.

Call her at her mother's house, Donald, something inside told him. You are helping her. You've always helped her and you want to continue to help her.

He walked to the phone and looked at it.

I have helped her, he thought. He saw her as they had been when they would talk after making love, lying together on the couch. She always felt freer to talk about herself at those times, and he had been able to get her to face more things then than she might have faced in years of therapy.

"Why do you undress in the corner like that, in secrecy, and then cover yourself up until . . . until you just can't any more?" he had asked.

"I just do it, that's all," she had replied rather testily.

He had kissed her on the cheek and played with her hair before he said, "You don't have to change as far as I'm concerned. I'm not unhappy with what you do. But you might be better served to go into your feelings more. There might be something in it for you."

She had nodded thoughtfully.

"Let your mind wander and let me know what you are thinking," he had said.

She had closed her eyes and then quickly opened them in surprise.

"I just saw a picture of my brother Billy."

"Go on."

"Once we shared a bedroom. My father had lost all his money a few years before and we had to move to a small apartment. I used to dress behind a screen, in a corner. I would face the wall the way I do here," she had said, smiling and making the obvious connection.

"If you had a screen why did you have to face the wall?"

Her face became red. "Because Billy would peek through the side of the screen."

"What did you do about it?"

"Nothing."

"Nothing?"

"I didn't want to make a fuss. He didn't see anything. I always had my back toward him."

"Your back is something to see."

She had patted his face playfully and smiled at him to shush.

"How old were you while all this was going on?"

"Oh, I was about twelve when we moved in and we stayed there till I was about sixteen and my father made a lot of money and we moved into the big house just before my sixteenth birthday."

"How did you feel about your brother peeking at you?"

"No harm in it. He was my brother."

"Did you like it?"

"No."

"Did you dislike it?"

Her form of resistance to his further probing was lovely. She had turned to him on the couch, stopping his lips with her fingers and pressing herself close to him.

But now he remembered that she had been in therapy with him almost a year and had never once gone near any of the material about her brother. How much longer in regular therapy would it have taken her to start looking into the little game she was playing with her brother? Two more years? Perhaps she never would have. Who could say positively that her experience with me has hurt her? Who could say positively that through this experience she is not freer, closer to the source of her neurosis? Oh, don't get me wrong. I'm not some damn quack who's going to write books and get on television openly advocating sexual intercourse with his patients. I am not standing here telling you that I did it for her. I did it for me, I know that. But what harm have I done her? What harm?

He was standing up now and he realized that he had been talking to Claude.

He sat on the bed and looked at the telephone. Should he call Patty at her parents' home?

If he did, then he would be entering into a whole new phase not only of this affair but of his life. He would be opening up new areas, facing dangers that he had never before believed existed. On the other end of the phone were extra dimensions to this thing that had only one dimension in his office. There were parents to be lied to, parents who could be indignant and threatening—her father sounded absolutely crazy.

His life had been so sheltered, so easy up to now, never any threats. . . . But he had not been happy. To hell with being sheltered!

He was going to have the courage to reach for something new! Hadn't he always felt as if he were an impostor, some sort of a spy-look-alike in a prefabricated skin? The core of his emotional self had never been in the life he was leading, and he had always known it. Isn't that why he had had the affair with Patty to begin with? Somehow hadn't he known that this little girl would lead him to his real self in some strange, circuitous way? He had secretly called her his soul mate. Wasn't that the real reason he had finally gone ahead with the affair?

And didn't he still want to travel to this newness and not stop in the middle of the journey leaving himself in torturous limbo?

If he stopped now and subjected this whole thing to analysis he could shore up his old personality; but, God damn it! he didn't want his old personality. He wanted something new—something alive and vibrant and different! If he was going back to the womb, then he was going there to pick up some things that were left behind—things that should not have been left behind, things he had really always needed. Are we so Goddamn correct to always stop our patients from going back to the womb?! God damn it! If we need to go, we need to go!

As he dialed the phone to Patty's parents' house, watching the roundness of the dial, he caught himself humming, "Love makes the world go 'round, Love makes the world go 'round."

A strange little Carmelita-like voice was singing it within

him and he saw an overweight ballerina turning around and around on a delicate music box—the bulging meat of the thighs mocking the Louis XIV lines of the music box. He chuckled the image away to concentrate completely on the call.

The phone at the other end was picked up and he heard a female voice say, "Hello." The voice was very much like Patty's but much lower and less squeaky. It could only be Patty's mother.

"Hello. Is Patty home?" Norton asked softly.

"Patty?" the woman answered dumbly yet suspiciously, as if she had never heard of such a person in her life.

"Yes, Patty," he replied more softly, not wanting to let too much of his voice into the phone.

"Patty doesn't live here any more. Patty lives in Connecticut," Patty's mother said as if she were answering a question that even the most ignorant child should know. "Who is this?" she continued harshly.

"I know she lives in Connecticut now, but wasn't she supposed to be in town this weekend?" Norton replied, his voice getting weaker, softer, younger and higher. When he had started to call girls for dates after he had gotten to college, this kind of thing would happen to his voice every time he talked to the girls' parents, as if to say to them, "Look, I'm no threat to your daughter, I'm just an innocent little boy." He would always try to get away with not identifying himself. Of course, meeting Helen at that fraternity dance had saved him from all that. From the first she had taken over, had made things easy for him. He never had to call her for a date. She would meet him on the campus with tickets to this or plans for that. He had spent a whole session on why his voice got so high and soft when he used to call girls and how meeting and marrying Helen had saved him from facing these fears. He had understood it perfectly then—so why was his voice so high now?

"Who is this?" Patty's mother persisted, not letting him

get away with avoiding the question. He decided that he might as well tell her who he was, otherwise there would be no way of getting information about Patty's whereabouts. He cleared his throat to make his voice lower as Patty's mother said, "Is this Dickie?"

Dickie! Dickie was a teen-age boy that Patty had dated before she was his patient. He flushed with the indignity of being mistaken for this pimply-faced, half-illiterate, semi-moronic teen-ager.

"This is Dr. Norton," he said, forcing his voice to be lower, more dignified.

As his voice went down her voice went up on a sliding scale from a harsh contralto to a high soprano.

"Oh, Dr. Norton! Patty's psychiatrist!"

"Yes," his voice now set and deep, comfortably hidden in his own identity. He was like an observer listening in, playing with the idea that if he were Verdi or Puccini he would have the material for an aria with these rising and lowering tones; ump-pa-pa, ump-pa-pa, went the first introductory chords.

"I was going to call you on Monday," she said. Then her voice dropped to the lower range. "We have something to talk about."

"Oh?" His voice went up somewhat. He sharply told himself to stop this voice-noticing nonsense and concentrate on the present danger. He braced himself for an accusation. Patty must have told her mother about him. He set himself not to sound shocked and to explain calmly to the woman that patients often distort things about their psychiatrists, and that all psychiatrists get accused at one time or another of having affairs with their patients.

"We have to get Patty to come back to you for treatment," she said.

An ally, not an enemy!

"I was concerned about the very same thing," he replied enthusiastically. "I had called her in Connecticut to find out if we could make some sort of arrangement to continue somehow. She was supposed to call me when she got into the city so that we could talk about it. Is she there?"

"Oh, I have wanted to talk to you, oh, so often," Patty's mother fairly cooed, ignoring his question as if it hadn't existed for her. He might have to be very patient if he were to get the information that he wanted. He leaned back and made himself more comfortable on the bed.

"I always thought you were such a wonderful psychiatrist. Patty got so much brighter and more responsible the minute she went to you. It was like a miracle. I don't know why she left you. I kept begging her to go back. And this proves it. You are so good. What other psychiatrist would take the trouble? Some of them are so cold, and here you are calling her up on a Saturday night of all things. My God, and I thought you were a beau when I picked up the phone"—squeals of self-mockery—"God bless you, doctor. . . . God bless you."

As if to lay to rest for good any idea in Patty's mother's mind that he was a beau, Norton made his voice go very deep as he said, "I would like to speak to her."

There was a pause, then a hushed whisper as she said, "Wait."

The phone was put down, and Norton waited to hear the sound of Patty's voice coming over the line. He didn't know what he was going to say—how he was going to sound— would her mother be nearby? Would he have to sound official? Would her mother pick up the extension and listen in? She was the type of woman who opened her children's mail, searched their rooms and listened to their phone conversations, Norton remembered from Patty's sessions. He would have to be very noncommittal; but if he were, would Patty be angry at him for his blandness? He was starting to sweat.

Suddenly a hushed voice said, "Hello." It was still her mother.

"I was just checking to see if her father was away. Thank

God he's left. He left the house without even telling me, but I don't care. I'm sure it's no secret to you what kind of man he is."

She paused for a comment, but of course Norton could say nothing because anything he had learned about Patty's father was clothed in confidentiality.

"Well, you know I can't comment—" he started to say, when she interrupted him.

"Oh, of course, isn't it wonderful; you're just like a priest."

"Did Patty go back to Connecticut yet?" Norton asked.

"No," she replied. "Oh, and I'm so nervous with those two in the house together. They're like oil and water, her father and her, especially since he found those pills."

She was sucking him into this. He had to ask her about what she had just said or run the risk of appearing too anxious about Patty's whereabouts.

"Pills?" he asked.

"She must have told you about that just before she went away, didn't she?"

Norton felt like a criminal taking the fifth amendment as he began to say, "Well, you know I can't divulge anything that has gone on in a session . . ."

"Oh, yes, of course, just like a priest, how wonderful . . ."

"If she's not in Connecticut . . . ?" he started to say in an effort to get back to Patty's whereabouts.

"I'm sure she told you about her father finding those BC pills, didn't she?" Patty's mother interrupted.

Now, Norton thought, I have to ask her what the fuck BC pills are.

"BC pills?" Norton asked.

"Birth control," Patty's mother answered, her voice suddenly hushed.

"Oh!"

"He's not a modern man. He made her leave home. There was nothing I could do about it. I didn't want her to go. He threw the pills into the toilet bowl and carried on and on until she had to leave. I'm sure she told you all about it, didn't she?"

Before Norton could issue his standard disclaimer she went on, "Oh, of course you can't tell me. Just like a lawyer-client relationship, isn't it? She must have spent a lot of time talking about me. I don't mind. I know I haven't always been right, but I'm learning. Did she tell you about the heart-to-heart we had just before she left? I took her out of the house away from her father. I didn't come on strong with her, because she'd told me that sometimes I come on too strong. She must have learned that from you, and you are right. I realized that. But this time I just forced myself to be silent and let her know that I wanted to help somehow without even saying a word. Nonverbal communication, right, doctor?"

"Yes," Norton said, resolved that he would have to conduct this conversation like a session before he could get the simple information that he wanted.

"'Mama,' she says to me, 'Mama, I'm involved with a man . . .'"

Norton caught his breath. Patty wouldn't have told her mother about him, would she? No, of course not; if Patty's mother knew he was the man she would not be so deferential.

"'Well, I figured that, honey, being I saw those pills and all. I'm a modern woman.' 'Well, mama, he's an older man and he's married.'

"'Oh, that's bad news, honey,' I told her right off the bat. What do *you* think, doctor?"

Norton wanted to hang up but if he did it would give the whole thing away. He could only listen and fake it through.

"Oh, well, I know you can't answer me. I know she must have talked to you a great deal about such a relationship. I mean, I don't know how you psychiatrists view these things.

I know you don't say what is right and what is wrong. But what do you think? Do you think it's right for a pretty little honey like my Patty in her early twenties to be fooling around with a married older man? You're a man of the world, Dr. Norton. You know what that son of a bitch is after and nothing more. He should drop dead for making my little girl so unhappy!"

She took a breath and waited a bit longer than usual for him to reply, and when he didn't she prompted, "What do *you* think, doctor?"

Norton was tired of feeling so frightened.

Well, fuck her, he told himself, she knows nothing. She can't hurt me. Why am I taking all this shit. Patty did not tell her who I was. I have nothing to be guilty about. She even said how much better her daughter had gotten.

"Listen," Norton said, strongly with a deep voice, "I really cannot even participate in a conversation like this about a patient. Now, please, all I want to do is talk to Patty. Is she there?"

There was a pause, and when Patty's mother spoke again her voice was deferential in a quieter, almost obsequious way.

"Oh, no, she's not here now."

Norton felt a surge of triumph in the obvious cowering of Patty's mother.

"Will she be back later?" He had her on the run, sticking spikes in her as she was fleeing.

"Well, I don't know," Patty's mother answered.

"You don't know?" Norton said sternly. Norton put the implication in the statement that if spoken would have come out as: "What kind of mother are you not to know if your daughter is going to be sleeping there or not?" He spiked her because she had tried to spike him with that "you know what that son of a bitch is after and nothing more" speech. Well, he could be the spokesman of middle-class morality, too, when it suited his purpose.

"Well, Patty's a big girl now. She has the keys and she can stay here if she likes. But she lives away from home now and I can't demand to know where she sleeps and all," Patty's mother was saying—defensively, of course. "After all, Patty's not a child any more. Do you have any children, doctor?"

Norton wished that she were a patient so he could turn that question around and ask the asker why she had asked that. But he couldn't. This was a social conversation he had gotten himself into.

"Yes, I have two children."

"Oh, two children? A boy and a girl?"

Oh, God, why am I still talking to this woman? "Two boys."

"Oh, two boys."

"Ages ten and twelve," Norton volunteered before she asked.

As Patty's mother ahhed over that, Norton realized that he was only hanging on to get some idea of how to get in touch with Patty again. Well, let me be direct, he decided.

"Well, look, it is very important that I at least talk to Patty while she is in the city this weekend. It would be in her best interest if I could see her. What would you suggest? Can I call her at some other number? Some friend's house?"

There was a strange note in Patty's mother's voice, a different note, almost innocent and yet beguiling as she said, "Well, I don't know, doctor. You see, the only thing she said to me was that if a man calls—*that* man—to tell him that she doesn't want to see him any more. She has finally wised up. She has finally seen that it is not good for her to have an affair with a married man with two children. You see, she told me the man she was involved with had two children."

A long dead pause on the phone.

"Dr. Norton? Are you still there? Are you by chance the man that Patty meant that message for, *Dr.* Norton?"

Perspiration was bursting from him—the mouthpiece of

the phone dripped as he could only dumbly pretend that he hadn't heard her properly.

"Huh?" he said, the weight beginning to leave his voice.

"Are you the man that Patty meant to leave that message for, Dr. Norton?" her mother repeated, level voice in middle octave.

"You mean Patty doesn't want any more sessions at this time?"

"Patty left no message for her psychiatrist. She only left a message for her married boy friend. Is that man you, *Dr. Norton?*"

"What are you talking about?" Norton said, damning his voice for skittering to high falsetto and not being a thundering baritone. He also objectively noted that his hand was beginning to shake.

"I want you to listen to me, *doctor.* I want you to leave my girl alone. How could you have done that to her, a man in your position, a man with the highest trust, like a priest or a lawyer?! How can she ever trust another doctor now?"

Norton couldn't talk, couldn't defend himself. He also couldn't hang up and discontinue the conversation. Every question, every accusation was like a lance driving him backward—younger and younger until he felt like an infant held dangling by his ankles being struck by a lancelike diaper pin. He could not answer Patty's mother. An infant. He could only listen.

"You're lucky that her father doesn't find out. Don't worry, I won't tell him. He would kill you—he would come to your office and kill you, that man would. He'd beat you up and then he would make you give him the fees back—the fees that he was paying you while you were doing what you were doing to his daughter! Are you going to give us a refund, *doctor?!*"

That ridiculous accusation suddenly snapped Norton and made him angry. He had always felt frustrated about Patty's fees. If Patty had been paying him he would not have accepted, but her father had been sending him checks, so he had no alternative but to accept. But how could he explain that to this crazy woman? He must get off the phone with as much dignity as he could. He forced his voice as low as possible.

"Please tell Patty that I called, and that if she ever wishes to resume treatment I will be available. Meanwhile, I will not call her again. Goodnight."

He paused, waiting for her to say goodnight so that the conversation would leave off with a social amenity.

"Drop dead," the woman said, and then the receiver was suddenly silent.

The phone was soaked with perspiration as he weakly put it back in its cradle.

As he sat there he could almost feel the little prop that was holding up his sanity as it slipped away, allowing an avalanche of rushing depression to bury him under its intolerable weight.

chapter seven

By the time he resumed his normal routine on Monday, he found that all he cared about was some moment-to-moment way to relieve his depression.

He decided to walk to the office from his apartment instead of taking the subway as he usually did, seeking to get involved with the freshness of the city in the morning as a diversion. As he began to walk he found himself anxiously searching the face of every man who happened to walk toward him, and he started to turn around, constantly, with an overwhelming fear that he was being followed. He soon realized that he was afraid that Patty's father might be after him—that in spite of her mother's saying she would not tell the father, she would anyway (can you trust someone like that?). There was a man coming toward him; the man was crossing the street, headed directly toward him, looking just the way her father might look—same age, same kind of morose belligerent features that he imagined her father to have. He tensed up. The man walked by, but Norton would have no more of this danger. He hailed a cab and got in, glad that the driver was black and could in no way be Patty's father.

When he arrived at the apartment house where he had his office, he viewed it as if it were a mine field. His office was on the twelfth floor. The doorman would let Patty's father come in because he would look respectable. Should he give the doorman a list of people to let in today and no one else?

No—he did not want to appear to be afraid. Besides, if the doorman tried to stop Patty's father there would be loud trouble. Patty's father would start shouting to the doorman and anyone else who might be around the reasons why he wanted to see the good doctor. That man was crazy!

The big danger could be expected in his waiting room. Patty's father was the kind of man who would be waiting there for him to walk in, and the minute he did he would come up to him and ask, "Are you Dr. Norton?" and if Norton said yes, Patty's father would slug him, and he'd be lying there in blood while Patty's father worked him over mercilessly, slugging him and making him bleed—leaving Norton a bloody pulp in his own waiting room—dancing fancy boxer steps over Norton's fallen body.

Norton had never gotten into a fight in his entire life, never really gotten close to getting into one. He wouldn't know how to handle himself. His father had left him helpless in a tough, hard-hitting world. As a boy he saw pictures all around his house of his father as a young man in fighting trunks with his boxing gloves, smug toughness and confidence. His father had fought in the Golden Gloves.

Why didn't he teach me? Norton thought, remembering the longing he had always had to be taught to fight. So much for the cliché of the hard-hat type trying to instill his version of masculinity in his son! Dad gave up on me, he felt betrayed because I was a fucking so-called genius. Now any fucking maniac can come to my office and beat the shit out of me, is that right, Dad?

He took the elevator to the eleventh floor and walked up one flight. He could see his office door from the stairwell through the glass part of the stairwell door. There was no one there; and suddenly he began to realize that he was almost enjoying this—it was a relief. His depression was lifting. He was feeling lightheaded over the prospect of what his first patient's reaction to this closed door would be. Norton always arrived at the office before this patient, a young executive—a smiling, handshaking man who could exude an almost magnetic friendliness that was getting him promotion after promotion but who suffered from severe migraines and terrible unending insomnia.

The man came up on the elevator and went to the door. Norton held his breath, watching every move with clinical excitement. At first the man experienced the locked door very calmly and rationally, ringing the bell, checking his watch, looking around to see what explanation could be gleaned from the empty hall. He waited nervously until the time that the session should have started. And then as it became apparent that Norton was late he began to become strangely calm. It was amazing to Norton how the entire body tension of the man changed, and he watched closely to see what he would do next. Suddenly the man slammed his fist into the center of the door and kicked it sharply; then he grabbed the handle and shook it, uttering sharp, guttural curse words. Norton noted it as the outward manifestations of the forces within the man causing inner manifestations of headaches and insomnia.

Norton ran down to the eleventh floor and caught the elevator to the twelfth. When the elevator door opened Norton found facing him a totally different man from the one he had just seen. His patient was all concerned friendliness, worrying whether anything had happened to Norton. It was remarkable. Norton apologized for being late as he opened the door to let the patient in. Norton locked his waiting room door from the inside as a precaution against the possible intrusion of Patty's father. It would be a new experience for each of his patients to have to ring the bell to get in, and he looked forward to working with it.

As this session went along Norton was disappointed that his patient was saying nothing about the fury he had just experienced. He was just going on, as he had done many times before, describing in detail the sleepless night he had just had.

"How did you feel about my being late and the door being locked?" Norton interrupted.

"Well, I was worried. It's not like you to be late, and I was afraid you might have had an accident or someone in your family might have been ill."

"What about yourself?"

"Well, I have an important conference this morning. I didn't want to be late for that."

"Were you angry?"

"No, of course not. Those things happen all the time, especially in this city with traffic and all."

"Really?"

"Really what?"

"You really weren't angry?"

"Mildly annoyed, if anything . . ."

"Mildly annoyed?"

"Yes, mildly annoyed."

"Why are you hiding your hand?"

"I'm not."

"It's between your legs. Is there anything wrong with it? May I see?"

The patient reluctantly showed Norton his red and swollen knuckles where he had slammed his fist against the door.

Norton felt the bones and determined that nothing was broken.

"How did that happen?"

There was a silence. The patient looked down for a long time, swallowed very hard, fighting tears, and said, "I slammed my fist against the door."

They had the best session they had ever had.

By Tuesday flashes of relief, sparked up by some of his patients' reactions to the closed door, were almost completely diminished. He had forgotten all about Patty's father.

He was now listening to one of his most depressed patients, a woman who could go on endlessly about how gloomy, dismal and hopeless her life was. As she droned on about how bad things were he found himself silently nodding with her in rhythmic agreement to each beat of despair. From now on, instead of the soaring, lovely music of Patty, which could pick him up and carry him along as if he were weightless, there was to be this chugging, heavy funeral march of despair, stooping him with its burden. Here was exemplified everything that he had now become, and he could not sit any longer—the sadness was rampaging through his body, causing rankling tensions and pains almost everywhere.

He stood up. "Excuse me," he said, and walked hurriedly to his closet. He couldn't get into it fast enough. He leaned against the door and shut his eyes, cataloguing the evidence of his depression. He checked his body out as if taking inventory in a store. The head heaviness, pain in the right thigh, pain in the back of the neck, difficulty in breathing. He was fascinated by the color of the antidepressant pills on the closet shelf, a cool mint green, and found refreshing relief just in looking at their pastel brightness. He leaned back, almost closing his eyes and relaxing his body against the wall. He took in only the cool mint green color and let that color enter him. His left hand reached up slowly and touched the pills and his right hand started to strike up a slow tempo as if conducting an orchestra. Instead, he was conducting the flow of the pill's magic cool-green stream. Its music, unheard and unsounded, flowed like a warm river through his fingertips, through his arm and into his body. The marvelous river of silent music was washing away his tensions! He picked up the tempo, and the flow went through his neck into his head and back down into the right side of his body. A vivid flash of floods that he had seen in newsreels sweeping cars and houses in their paths zipped through his mind. He increased the tempo; faster and faster, his right hand cascading the river down to his right inner thigh . . . lower and stronger . . . lower and stronger with a downward-sweeping crescendo. The pain in his thigh was swept away! The river danced through his body—mint green and bouncy! He slowed it and swished it around, savoring his mastery over it.

Mastery—that was it—that was the answer—if he could master his feelings—if he could wash away this depression—be in total control of his mind and body, then he would be free. Patty could leave him—he could have dozens of Carmelitas—hundreds of morose women like this present patient, but it wouldn't matter; he would be able to legislate to himself how he would feel, and that is all that counts in this whole fucking world: how you feel inside—everything else is bullshit!

He would have to go back out now.

He would have to let the river slowly run back into the pill.

He conducted it in slowly, very slowly, taking soundings of each part of his body as the river flowed away from it.

Yes, his right thigh was fine now . . . his intestinal area was greatly eased . . . weight no longer so oppressive on his chest (but still there somewhat) . . . neck feeling much better . . . head very cleared . . .

But as the last of the river flowed back into the pill the pain returned to his right thigh and his intestines were tightening up again . . .

"We were just lying there on the floor of my apartment listening to Dylan—you know, Bob Dylan? I had put up candles and incense, and the whole thing gave me a feeling that I was in another world—or better yet, I was in the world that this world should be. You know what I mean, doctor? I looked over at Peter lying there beside me, realizing that he was part of the whole scene . . . the music, the incense, the candlelight . . . and I felt that I was outside of it and I wanted to be part of it too, part of him, part of everything beautiful. I wanted him so much, more than I ever wanted anything in my life. We got real close and he kissed me and I kissed him. It was beautiful, I felt part of his beauty. But then Peter stopped kissing me and I could see that he was going to sleep. I—I put my hand on his knee and I started to go up his leg. I knew that what I was doing was terrible but I was going to take a chance, expose myself, make myself vulnerable—that's what you're supposed to do, right, doctor? Peter stopped my hand just before it got to you know where, and he said, 'Baby, you're still too fat,' and he turned over on his side and went to sleep."

Norton saw himself as audience watching this scene. He loved the line, "Baby, you're still too fat." He put it into the voice of Bob Dylan and he heard the Dylan twang dart that out. "Baby, you're still too fat." . . .

On Tuesday night Norton had stopped off at a local pet store and had bought a little laboratory mouse. He bought it to use with Carmelita at her Wednesday session. The idea had helped to get him through the night.

It's just what she needs, he thought, just like the locked doors have helped all my patients, the little mousey will help this one. Instead of her dealing with this Peter-coming-into-therapy business, she will deal with her feelings around the little mousey. He had concealed it in the bookshelf on the wall that Carmelita always stared at in her session.

"I wasn't hurt by what he said because I realized that he was right. I realized that he was only saying that for my own good. He didn't want me to settle for small results, he wanted me to continue to improve, and he knew that if he rewarded me at that point, I might settle."

He noticed that not only was she showing a significant weight loss but also she was cleaner now. Her makeup was put on more sparingly and her clothes were not stained and dirty. He put his left hand into his collar, touching his not perfectly clean shirt . . . no clean shirts left and he just had not been able to bring himself to arrange for laundry yet . . . this same shirt the third day in a row . . . a certain beefiness at his chin . . . putting on a bit of weight lately . . .

"Doctor," she said, abruptly changing her tone. "He will see you. Can he come at my next session?"

I have it, he told himself, the fat fool is furious at Peter for rejecting her and she wants to punish him by putting him in the straitjacket of therapy. Peter does not need a thera- pist; a therapist needs Peter. Peter sleeps through turmoil and I meet turmoil more than half way. Peter is a superb artist; and will I ever be a Freud or a Jung or anything but a fee-collecting New York psychiatrist, no better and no worse than any of them? Peter is loved by a multitude of friends and I could not call anyone to sit down and have a beer with. Ahh, yes, for every Garden of Eden there is a snake, and I am that snake and Peter is Adam and you are treacherous Eve, you fat bitch, trying to deliver Adam from Paradise. Come on, little mousey, strut your stuff. Don't be shy; come on out.

"What do you hope to gain if Peter goes into therapy with me?" he asked.

"I want to save a worthwhile person."

"Save him from what?"

"His own neurosis."

"Do you think he's neurotic?"

"Yes . . . we're all neurotic . . ."

"Everyone is neurotic?"

"Except you, doctor."

"By saying that everyone is neurotic, aren't you making it easier for yourself to get involved with a neurotic person?"

"I see what you mean. He's too neurotic. I should look for a normal man and not try to change neurotic men. Oh, yes, I always try to do that . . . then you think I shouldn't be involved with him, is that right?"

He looked up at the bookcase and saw the little mouse's tail moving slightly behind the volume of Freud's Dreams. He thought about what must be in the mouse's mind. He has gotten used to his new environment, the voices that he has been hearing are not new and strange to him any more. He has been stuck for a long time and now he is ready to step out and expand his world as I have been trying to expand my world. He will step out in front of the Freud's Dreams, and he will cause a bit of commotion and run a risk of being hurt; but he has no choice, as I had no choice. Come on, little mousey, there may be pain and depression ahead for you, but you've got to do it because you've got to do it; come on, little baby, don't be shy.

Having received no answer to her previous question, Carmelita was continuing, "But if Peter comes to you and you cure him of his neurosis, that would be all right, wouldn't it, doctor?"

"Why do you want Peter to come to me? Why not another psychiatrist?"

"Oh, you're such a wonderful doctor. I want nothing but the best for Peter."

The mouse darted out from behind the Freud and walked in front of the books, sniffing and slowly looking around. Carmelita's head was turned sideways and backwards as she tried to address herself to him more directly. Norton said, "Umm-huh," and was silent, waiting for her to turn around and see her new friend.

Carmelita turned around and faced the mouse directly. Norton tensed himself, waiting for her reaction, but she just went on.

"You've helped me so much. I would never have been able to lose the weight I've lost, and I've been so much more open with people I meet and so much less lonely. Oh, don't get me wrong, I'm not perfect yet. I know I have a long way to go . . ."

If you were better adjusted, you fat bitch, you would see the fucking mouse right in front of your eyes. Move around, little mouse, stop sitting there listening to this drivel.

As if responding to Norton's thought, the little mouse glided past the anatomy books.

". . . but I feel that at the end of the tunnel there will be some light. I feel—" Carmelita stopped dead. Norton held his breath.

"Doctor," she whispered urgently.

"Yes."

"Doctor, there's a mouse on your bookshelf."

"What?" he said.

"I don't want to point at it, but there is a mouse on the bookshelf."

"Which bookshelf?" There were many bookshelves in this office.

"The one facing me," she said, her voice on a rising tide of panicky nervousness.

"Ahh, yes, I see the mouse," he said, rising.

Carmelita jumped quickly on the couch, fixing her knees tightly together. She bunched her skirt and held it at the kneecaps. Norton walked slowly to the mouse on the bookshelf.

"Nothing to be afraid of," he said. "It's just a laboratory mouse. There's a fellow on this floor does experiments with them and once in a while one escapes."

"Kill it! Kill it!"

"Oh, no, you wouldn't kill a laboratory mouse. They're clean, no danger in them."

Norton put his hand on the bookcase behind the mouse and was slowly sneaking up on it to grasp it when she shouted, "Don't touch it, doctor. It'll bite you!"

That shout together with the approaching hand so scared the mouse that he jumped off the bookcase onto the floor and scampered under the couch.

Carmelita screamed and buried herself into the wall, closing her eyes and bending her knees further, wailing as if a guillotine were slowly descending on her.

"Ohhh . . ."

"Look how frightened you are," Norton said. "Why are you so frightened?"

"Get the mouse!"

"We must use everything that becomes available to us in therapy. Tell me quickly what thoughts come into your mind right now."

"Where is the mouse?"

"On the floor, under the couch."

"Are you sure it's not on the couch?"

"You don't believe me?"

"I didn't say that . . . I'm frightened . . ."

"That's the point. You're frightened out of all proportion to the danger. We can strike therapeutic gold. Now calm down, calm down . . ."

He caught her panicky eyes in his, which made her stop her moaning.

"Has it moved?" she asked.

"No."

"Will it climb up on the couch and get me?"

"What do you mean, 'get me'?"

"You know, will it . . . get up my leg and . . ."

"And what?"

"Oh, doctor, please! Just catch it! Catch it!"

"Now listen carefully," Norton said urgently. "The mouse cannot harm you. It is more frightened of you than you are of it. It carries no vermin. I am going to take off my shoes to show you that there is nothing to be afraid of."

Norton quickly took off his shoes and socks.

"Now, look," he said, raising one foot almost to her head. She looked tentatively. He put his foot down.

"Would I be walking around barefoot if there were any danger? Would I?"

"No," she said.

"Do you believe me?"

"Yes, doctor, I believe you . . . but the mouse . . . ?"

"Forget the mouse. Quickly!" Norton loved the sharp, crisp command in his voice. He felt marvelous.

"What image comes to your mind right now? Right now!"

"I see my father, oh, it doesn't make sense."

"Don't worry about it making sense, just keep on. You see your father."

"I am just a little girl lying in bed and my father has come home. He is drunk again and I am scared."

"You're scared, go on, why are you scared?"

"The mouse!" She suddenly yelled as the little creature scampered out from under the couch and ran under his desk.

"Never mind the mouse. Why were you afraid? Would he beat you?"

"No. My father never beat me."

"Then why should you be frightened?"

"I didn't like to see him drunk."

"What happened when he came back drunk?"

"I don't know, I forget. Oh, doctor, please do something about the mouse."

"This is resistance. You are getting to something important. Go on."

"What if the mouse bites you on your toe?"

He walked over to the desk and put his foot under it. There was no movement from the mouse.

"See? There is no danger or else I would not put my toe there." He walked back to the couch. "Continue."

Carmelita just hugged the wall, putting her face to it and being silent for a moment. She was concentrating.

Yes, Carmelita, use your therapy, piece it all together, hook it up and understand it. Even become an expert like me if you can, but you'll still be unhappy. I am the master of all this shit and I am still miserable.

"I see him sitting on the bed with me. I pretended to sleep. My covers were on the floor and I was wearing a little nightie. He would rub my leg and look at me sort of funny. He would rub my leg up and down from the ankle to the knee at first. Then his hand would go over my knee and go all the way up my thigh almost to—almost to you know where—" she suddenly turned around to Norton, her eyes popping. "Just like I am afraid the mouse is going to do. Just like I am afraid the mouse is going to run up my legs to you know where. Doctor, I have it. That's why I'm so frightened of the mouse!"

"Why haven't you left the room if you are so frightened?"

"I don't know."

"Why were the covers off your bed when your father came home drunk?"

"Huh?"

"Don't you see a connection between the two questions?"

Her eyes widened further.

"You mean I wanted it? I wanted it to happen? Oh, doctor, right now I saw an image of Peter's hand running up my leg. What does that mean? Oh my God, maybe I wanted to seduce my father! Maybe I do want the mouse to run up my leg! Could that be possible?!"

"Our time is up now."

"It is?"

"We have struck gold. We will mine it in other sessions. Go quickly, leave the mouse to me."

Carmelita slowly got off the couch, her gaze fixed under the desk, waiting for the mouse to make a move. When her feet touched the floor she said, "Doctor, can I help you catch the mouse?"

An expedition—this will be an expedition, an adventure with Captain Norton at the helm.

"Empty that wastepaper basket," he commanded.

Carmelita immediately obeyed without a trace of fear. She picked up the basket and dumped the papers on the floor. He motioned her to follow him, to tiptoe to the desk.

"Stay right here," he whispered, pointing to the front of the desk. "I'll get behind the desk and shoo him out. When I do, trap him with the basket. Careful not to kill the little thing."

"All right, I'll be careful."

"Are you frightened?"

"No. I've worked it through."

"Marvelous."

Norton crouched behind the desk and bent down to look under it. The mouse was trying to hide behind a leg of the desk.

"Ready?"

"Ready when you are, doctor," she said resolutely.

He slowly put his hand under the desk, and when it almost got to the mouse, the mouse charged out directly at Carmelita.

"Aghhh!" she screamed, dropping the wastepaper basket,

scurrying back onto the couch, standing on it and hugging the wall.

When Norton looked up he saw the mouse in a corner looking straight at Carmelita, who was looking straight at it, perspiration dripping from her face.

"I thought you had worked it through," Norton chided. "All right, our time is up now. I'll catch the mouse, don't worry."

"Are you angry with me for letting you down?"

"We'll continue next time." He walked to the couch and put his hand out for Carmelita to take. She clutched it and he led her quickly past his wonderful little friend, opening the door for her to get out.

Just as he was closing the door on her she stopped and said, "I'll bring Peter with me on my next session."

He felt a sense of helpless frustration. Nothing could deter her, she must have her way. He wanted to say no. He wanted to say that she couldn't bring Peter but he felt that even if he did it wouldn't do any good. So he said nothing as she closed the door and went away.

He turned and looked at the mouse, thinking how small it was; thinking that even after it scared the elephant it was still a mouse, that even if it could press a button to blow up the whole universe it would still be a mouse, and only a mouse.

He squatted on the floor and tried to look the mouse in the eye, but the mouse wasn't particularly interested. He lay down and looked at the mouse on the same level. He squeaked and the mouse looked at him briefly, so he squeaked again but the mouse looked away. The mouse was not his friend. They couldn't have a beer together and talk about what they had just done to old fat-ass—it made Norton sad, and he remembered that he had his appointment with Claude and it wouldn't do to be late. He reached over and picked up his friend. No, he thought sadly, not his friend, but a little mouse. He put him back in his container and left for his session.

He would take it with him to Claude's and let it out in the woods—let it roam freely. Then perhaps it would find the pond and crawl in and sink down somewhere beneath the surface and find the source.

But it wouldn't make any difference at all, Norton reflected, looking at the thing in the container. Even if it found the source it would still be a mouse.

chapter eight

NORTON was very apprehensive all during his drive to see Claude. He wanted to get an answer from Claude about Patty without posing a question.

Should he see her?

Should he try to forget her?

Conversations bounced around in his mind. He would invent hypothetical patient situations close to his own and try to catch an attitude from Claude.

He invented a teacher who was having an affair with a student and began posing questions to Claude, when he realized that this situation wasn't the same as his own. He even tried a priest with a parishioner and discarded it because that wasn't quite the same thing either.

Just before he arrived he saw that there was nothing quite the same and that furthermore he was trying too hard—straining too much.

His trouble was that he lacked faith.

Yes, faith, faith in the power of the universal unconscious.

Yes, the answer would occur to him in this session. Something would happen. He would go in without one prepared thing on his mind, and something magical and wonderful would happen, some analytical miracle, some subconscious awakening that would give him the direction he needed. Just trust the subconscious, it knows the way. The inner invisible spring of peace sceped into him and he knew that the unraveling was near if he would just trust the subconscious. Yes, all answers lay there.

As he prepared to lie down he noticed that no head rest had been set up for him. Claude has gotten a bit careless, he thought, he must be getting old.

Claude was saying something.

"Before we begin our session, I want to talk to you about something that happened this week."

Norton looked directly at Claude, studying his face for the first time in a long while. Claude must be reaching sixty by now, and his wrinkles are more pronounced. He is still very alert and peaceful looking. He has nice gray hair. I wonder what I'll look like when I'm his age? I'd better not grow too fat, stay slim just as he is.

"I received a phone call from your wife this week," Claude said, and he continued to talk about the call.

Norton nodded but did not listen to the rest of what Claude was saying. He almost said something like, "Oh, how nice, give her my regards," but he stopped himself in time.

He had better focus on what was happening ... make a conscious effort to get with it or else he would never find out what to do about Patty. Meanwhile, Claude was talking and Norton couldn't pick out what he was saying.

Yet he couldn't admit that he hadn't been listening.

Claude had stopped talking and obviously was waiting for Norton to reply to what had been said. Norton felt mildly annoyed at Helen for trying to disturb his analytical relationship with Claude and he felt that Claude was overstepping his role as an analyst to even take the call. He looked around the office for the head rest so that he could lie on the couch and have his session.

"What are you looking for?" Claude asked.

"The head rest. I'd like to start my session now."

"Did you hear what I said before?" Claude asked evenly.

"Yes," Norton replied.

There was a long silence.

Norton saw the head rest at the other end of the couch.

"There it is," he said to Claude.

"I didn't put it up because I wanted to discuss the content of what Helen told me in a non-analytical manner."

That frightened Norton.

He knew that analysis is not appropriate for people undergoing psychotic episodes. Claude might diagnose him as having a psychotic episode at this very moment. If he were diagnosing himself as a patient, that is what he might put down. But of course he knew differently. The doctor inside knows more than the doctor outside. But the doctor outside doesn't know that. He had better give Claude what he wanted or there might be some difficulty. Claude might want to hospitalize him.

"Yes," Norton said, turning to Claude reasonably, "I see what you mean. You have received information about a patient—you see I can call myself a patient now—outside of the analytical relationship and so you choose to deal with it outside of the analytical relationship as well. I think that is an excellent decision."

"Well, frankly, at this stage, Donald, I don't care how we deal with it as long as we deal with it."

"Yes, that teaches me a great deal, Claude . . . ritual develops from need, but all too often the ritual persists long after the need is diminished—"

"Donald," Claude interrupted, "I would like to talk about the phone call."

"Oh, I'm sorry, was I running off? I just do that sometimes, don't I, doctor? Yes, Helen called you, yes . . ."

Norton looked closely at Claude. Was he angry? Getting furious? Feeling bad because he hadn't told him all about his soap opera problems with his wife? Listen, doc, I didn't come here to work out middle-class-morality problems, he was saying to himself out of the side of his mouth, fancy dancing in a fighting ring with huge Golden Gloves on, jabbing and left-hooking his way to the championship of inner peace and perfected psyche. Yeah, I got more important fish to fry . . . a psyche to woik out . . . inner-peace obstacles to KO. Yeah! Yeah!

Stop being silly, he told himself, you've got to concentrate on what's going on or else he's going to hospitalize you. "What did Helen say to you?" he asked.

"She called me because she felt alarmed at the way you have been acting lately. She told me that she left you because you had told her you didn't want to have sex with her any more, that you had found someone else for that. She told me she has tried a number of times to talk with you about the future but you refused to discuss it. I made no comment to her one way or the other. I just listened to the information she gave me and said goodbye. Her purpose was to get you to face the situation. That is not my purpose for bringing it up."

"Oh?"

"What you do with your personal life is your business, Donald. I make no judgments. I am only concerned that all this has been going on while you've been in analysis and you have not brought it up. Frankly, that seems astounding to me. It is an almost acrobatic feat of resistance ... and it alarms me ... I would like to find out why you haven't brought any of this material into the analysis ..."

Claude paused, waiting for Norton to answer.

Norton did not know what to say. Should he tell the truth —namely, that he did not need to bring it up because it was no problem, because it was going exactly the way he wanted it to go—except for a few minor adjustable things? No, that would sound very defensive and not quite rational. Should he tell him that he was going to bring it up at this very session? No—that would sound too phony. If he wanted to get out of this session without Claude trying to hospitalize him, he'd better do it the way he knew Claude wanted it done.

"I was frightened, Claude," he said.

Ah, see how his face perks up. This is the kind of stuff he wants to hear.

"I was afraid you would disapprove. I kept telling myself that I ought to talk about it at each session but then I just couldn't get to it, and the more I couldn't get to it the more guilty and silly I felt about not being able to get to it. I mean ... I knew that after a while if I started to talk about the whole thing, one of the questions you would ask would be why I hadn't spoken about it sooner."

"That's right."

"So you understand how that kind of thing builds up, don't you?" He was asking for Claude to agree that it was understandable, but Claude just waited for him to go on. They were back in the analytical relationship now. Soon he would be able to lie down on the couch and find out what to do about Patty.

"Can I lie down?" he asked Claude.

Norton could see that Claude was a bit flustered, undecided. "I want to start dealing with this whole thing now," Norton said, compiling more things to tell Claude that he knew Claude wanted to hear so that Claude would allow him to lie down. Next he was about to tell Claude that it would be easier for him to talk about his guilt if he didn't have to face him. Freudians love that shit.

Claude picked up the head rest and placed it on the couch and Norton promptly lay down.

Now that he was there he did not know what to do. How could he talk about Patty without revealing to Claude that she was a patient? He could lie about who she was, but lying could be easily detected by someone as sharp as Claude.

"What are you thinking?" Claude asked after a while.

"Kind of blank," he replied.

"Really?"

Does he see what I am thinking? Does he know that I am hiding?

"It's difficult for me. I feel kind of frightened... don't quite know where to start..."

Where could he start? He couldn't start anywhere. All roads led to anger—Claude's anger and condemnation. Patty was a patient and you do not make love to a patient. Period. Claude could never view his love for Patty objectively.

Love.

Love for Patty.

Did he say love?

Did you say love, Donald?

There was a little knowing friendly giggle somewhere within him and the voice behind that giggle said, Of course you said love, you silly boy. Isn't it about time you realized it?

He asked himself calmly, Do you love this girl, Donald Norton, M.D., boy psychiatrist, Phi Beta Kappa, hard-hat genius?

Do you love Patty?

Yes. Yes I do. I love her. I her love.

Love her I?

I do.

Do I?

Do. Do.

Stop being silly.

Think.

My entire problem unraveled. I loved her and I did not want to accept the love. I thought I was going crazy but all those aches and pains and depressions were nothing but normal lover's feelings because my love had left me.

He was free.

Yes, Donald, you are free, the something within him chimed in—there was perfect harmony. He knew what to do now. You must pursue your love, you silly boy—you must pursue your love as quickly as possible. She might need you at this very moment.

Get in your car and drive up to Connecticut without a moment's delay, the something directed.

Yes, without a moment's delay, he echoed.

In her sadness she might be reaching out for another and you could lose her. She is your soul mate . . . your one and only, it went on.

My soul mate . . . my one and only. I could be losing her.

"Is my time up now?" he asked Claude.

"No," Claude replied.

"I have to go. I should have told you when I walked in, but this has to be a short session. I have somewhere to go."

He stood up.

"Donald," Claude said. "You can't go now."

So that's it, Norton suddenly saw; Claude had some sort of sanitarium in the house. A hospital for flipped-out psychiatrists. Probably on the second floor. Claude would try to prevent him from going to Patty. Claude was no match for Norton physically. Norton would never hurt Claude. He loved Claude. He revered Claude. Claude was one of the kindest most gentle men in the whole world, and Norton knew that Claude would only act out of what he felt were the purest motives. But Claude would be wrong to try to restrain him now.

He probably has attendants upstairs waiting for some kind of signal. Norton would be all right if he could keep Claude from pressing some kind of button that he must have concealed somewhere. He looked around for it.

Claude stood up and gently put his hand on Norton's arm. "Donald," Claude said, "I think you're going through a pretty rough time now. I'm very worried about you."

Could Claude be stronger than he looks? Norton thought, looking at Claude's hand lying gently on his arm. Is he going to try something?

"Donald, I would like you to stay here with me for a while. It's very peaceful up here, you'll get a chance to relax and we can talk—no analysis—just talk, get things off your chest, see what's really happening . . ."

There it is.

Claude wants to hospitalize me.

And this is the hospital!

Norton moved his arm gently away from Claude's hand. He moved a couple of steps toward the door.

"I don't know . . . I'm not supposed to take my vacation till fall. Helen's arranged a cruise or something. We had planned on staying in the city all summer. City is really a remarkable place in the summer if you plan right."

"Helen isn't with you any more, Donald. It's not a good idea for you to be alone."

"I didn't want her to leave, you know. It was her idea entirely."

"Oh?" Claude said, opening the door and leading Norton out to the living room.

Norton kept his eye on Claude every second. He would

run if he saw Claude give a signal. He felt his jacket pocket for the keys to his car and mentally went through the physical acts of running, taking the keys from his pocket with his left hand while he opened all the house doors with his right hand, then jumping down the steps into his car on the driveway and starting the engine while two big attendants would charge out of the house chasing him.

One of them would be a big black man with an Afro and the other would be a college-type white football player. The kind of attendants who loved a scrape and loved to talk about the nuts on the wards over a couple of beers. Wouldn't they be delighted that one of the nuts was a shrink! Well, fuck them!

"I have an enormous case load these days, Claude. I really can't just stop right now. I do need a rest, but it'll take me a little time to rearrange the patients . . . some of them really can't be stopped so abruptly . . . you know what I mean. It's bad enough when you leave for a normal vacation, but an abrupt one causes a great many problems . . ."

"Donald," Claude said levelly, "I don't think you're in shape to treat patients right now. I think you have to sort things out in your own mind before you can help other people sort things out in theirs."

Claude was walking toward a large, comfortable-looking chair in the living room and he motioned for Norton to sit in a chair equally comfortable-looking that was opposite it.

"Claude," he suddenly interrupted, "we know so much about mental illness, so how can we get ill?"

"We know a great deal about mental illness, except our own," Claude replied. "We don't think of what we are going through as being ill, so we don't act on what we know. It's one thing to know and it's another to act. We are subject to the same forces that we treat in our patients, only sometimes we think we're above it."

Claude sat down in his armchair and put his hands on the

arm rests. He motioned for Norton to sit in the other chair. The armchair that Claude wanted him to sit in was a trap. The armchair was to be his prison, somehow enfolding him and locking him up. He stood there, disobeying Claude's invitation.

What would Claude do next?

Claude's right hand was slipping slowly from the top of his armchair to the side.

Was there a button concealed there?

Yes.

Claude would press the button and the two attendants would rush down from upstairs.

Norton turned swiftly and headed for the door to freedom.

"I have to go now," he shouted back as he opened the door and leaped down the stairs onto the grass and then onto the driveway, his key already out in his left hand just as he had planned. He scooted into the car, turned on the ignition and was on the road . . . exhilarated by the action . . . delighted in the results. He looked back and, seeing no one pursuing him, congratulated himself on his total awareness of what was happening.

chapter nine

THE police car was catching up to him. He watched it in the rear-view mirror as it grew from a little speck with a protuberance on top that identified it as an official car to a full-grown State Police vehicle. Claude must have called the highway police and informed them that a dangerous lunatic was loose.

He became angry at Claude—resentful of the betrayal. One psychiatrist doesn't do that to another psychiatrist! Norton would not have handled it that way. He would have recognized that the patient was not dangerous and did not need to be detained by the police. He would never go back to Claude again. Claude did not have a leg to stand on.

There was no legal basis for Norton to be detained. Norton was a doctor too. He had identification to prove it.

The car was coming up fast, slipped into the left lane preparing to pull alongside Norton. There was one officer in the car. Sunglasses and heavy young face.

I have an emergency call to make in Connecticut, officer, he prepared himself to say. I am a doctor and I have a patient who needs me very badly in Connecticut. You can check if you like, here's her name.

Oh, that's no good. What if the officer checked? Patty would tell the officer that she hadn't called him. She would not tell the officer that she needed him desperately because she really didn't know it yet. That's why he had to see her, to let her know that she needed him desperately. It is an emergency for her, he would tell the officer. You see, I am a psychiatrist and we know these things. If she does not have me she will get into desperate trouble—drugs, God knows what else, don't you see, officer? It all may be taking place at this very moment. She might be making commitments that will hound her the rest of her life. . . .

He won't believe all that. Sounds crazy, Norton reflected. But I have done nothing. It is my word against Claude's. Just because Claude is a psychoanalyst and I am a psychiatrist it doesn't mean that they will believe Claude before they believe me. Cops wouldn't know the difference anyway.

Yes, he would say nothing and play it by ear.

He tensed himself as the police car pulled beside him.

The car whooshed on by him without the officer even glancing his way.

He watched it ahead of him, speeding away.

Of course it was a trick.

The officer was trying to make him feel that he was safe. Norton checked his speedometer and saw that he was going over seventy, so he slowed his car down gradually—if he did it too fast the officer would know that he was doing it for the officer's sake. He did not want to let the officer know that he had that much power over him. If you let them know you are afraid and that they can control your actions, then they've got you, Norton counseled himself.

The police car was disappearing now. The danger was passing temporarily, but he would be alert from here on in—they might be circling him, one car in front and one behind, waiting for him to incur the most minor infraction so that they could arrest him.

Claude would not want him to see Patty.

But nothing was going to stop him.

Nothing.

What was he going to say to her when he saw her?

He must plan.

He must win her.

"You must win your own true love, Donald," a voice sprang out of him. He laughed at himself. God, I sound like ol' Carmelita.

He fixed his rear-view mirror so that he could see his face in it, and he twisted his mouth and arched his head the way she arched hers, admiring his imitation and loving the way his voice had just the right soap opera throb as he said, "Oh, Donald, you are bitten by the love bug. Cupid has shot his arrow and has pierced your heart. True love must and will conquer all!"

He switched, becoming himself in a session—mock-serious face, deep theatrical voice. "Yes, fat-ass—bitch—elephant cunt! Could not this true love you speak of be nothing but true neurosis? What could a fat-ass—which is what you are, I am officially telling you—know about true love?"

He switched back to Carmelita. "Your great mission in life will be to help your loved one to conquer her neurosis—lose yourself in her problem. You are such a good doctor. Even when you did your little mousey on me, you naughty boy, you were so brilliant. Remember, in order to find yourself you must lose yourself."

"In order to find yourself you must lose yourself. Very good, elephant ass."

"Oh thank you, thank you. You can do it, doctor. And remember ... when you have your true love, you will be a fulfilled, worthwhile human being."

Another car had come up beside him. The driver was gaping at this strange-looking man in the big car with an MD license plate who was making weird faces and talking to himself. He was a young newlywed who worked for a small upstate bank and was experiencing difficulty finding things to talk about with his new bride. He was relishing everything that was happening and making sure to remember every detail of what he could make out so that he would have enough material to get him through the evening. It was amazing how the man in the car (could he really be a doctor?) could almost seem like a woman one moment, with those feminine head motions, and then snap into a man in the next moment. He wondered what he was saying. Was this guy flipping out? Maybe he should stop and call the highway police? No, why get involved with that crap? ...

Suddenly the guy in the MD car turned around and saw him staring. The guy's eyes blazed with anger; the young man felt terrified. This guy is a loony, he thought. Is he going to crash his car into mine? I better get the fuck out of here. The guy in the MD car was shouting something at him. The young man could read his lips as he put his foot heavily on the gas pedal and zoomed away.

The guy in the MD car was shouting, "Fuck off! Fuck off! Fuck off, Johnny, fuck off!"

Norton laughed triumphantly as the young schmuck raced off in his dinky Plymouth like a scared rabbit. . . . His father had beat the shit out of someone once. He had seen it from the screened porch. His father had danced around, moving so gracefully in spite of his bit of a paunch. The man on the floor had been downed with a left hook . . . not daring to get up . . . his father just dancing until the man cried uncle. His mother had raced out of the house and grabbed his father's shoulders and pushed him into the house, furious that all this had been going on in front of the boy.

". . . in front of the child!" the boy could hear her whispering vehemently at his father, who had gone sullenly into the house without a word. The goddamn fucking injustice of that! To conquer and not to triumph! His mother came to him with her glory-robbing arms around him, babbling about love and kindness and it being bad to fight and all that shit, and he had nodded and agreed with his mother; but still he could not get out of his head the picture of his dad left-hooking that son of a bitch to the ground. All the love and kindness in the world could never feel as good as he felt when he saw his father dancing over that big fuck! . . . Now, should he race after that young punk in the dinky Plymouth and teach him a fuckin' lesson? Stop him on the side of the road and show him a thing or two?

Well, maybe just scare the son of a bitch a little bit.

Norton put his foot down heavily on the accelerator and started to catch up to the other car. He was excited as the dinky Plymouth drew closer to him.

The young man looked over his shoulder and saw Norton coming up fast; and he turned around in sheer panic, put his foot on the pedal and zoomed off at his maximum speed.

Norton again laughed triumphantly as he saw the car disappear down the road like some animated cartoon character fleeing from a mighty predatory menace.

He was satisfied.

He had conquered, he had triumphed.

"Love and kindness! Love and kindness, baby!" he yelled, not caring if there were ten million cops hiding out to get him, feeling carefree and invincible.

Soon the sign for Patty's town appeared, announcing that he was near his destination.

He must plan.

What was he going to say to her?

He would tell her he loved her.

He would tell her he wanted to see her—be her man—her lover.

Yes.

All in the open now. No hiding. No married-man business. No patient-doctor relationship.

He saw her on his arm walking into a restaurant. So young and so pretty. Smiling, loose, relaxed now; a gracious, pretty, poised lady, his lady—yes, this tight little pretty girl now his gracious lady. He saw himself introducing her to his colleagues. Because of him there now existed this lovely person. He couldn't tell them, of course. But he wouldn't have to. *He* would know. And then of course she would always love him and only him, making love freely, not ashamed of anything about herself. He saw her as she had been the last time they had made love. He remembered vividly how her nipples had hardened at his touch. She had begun to respond—really respond that last time, moaning, loosening up; how marvelous to see her nipples rise, her being rise to a crescendo like a fine orchestra, the defenses of her body and her mind slipping away, eroding . . .

That was why she left him!

It all became clear to him.

She had become absolutely terrified at her own responses. She had arranged for her father to find those birth-control pills which caused the fight which made it right for her to leave home.

The reason she did not want to see him any more was not because she didn't want to see him any more but because she wanted to see him too much. More than she felt she could handle. It was her defenses that didn't want to see him, not Patty herself!

Very common, typical symptom.

He must make her realize that!

He loved her and he must make her realize that her not wanting to see him was a symptom of her neurosis!

"This is my challenge," he found himself saying out loud. "To save her from her own defenses." He imagined saying that to ol' Carmelita on the couch and her turning her fatness around to listen to him. "Can true love conquer all? Oh, Carmelita, wise, wondrous woman of the ages, will you be right? Can true love conquer all?"

"Oh, yes, doctor," he said, giggling in that "of course, silly boy" way of hers and quickly looking around at both his sides to make sure that no other car was near. "True love will conquer all—never fear."

He pulled into the first gas station he saw when he drove into town. A middle-aged short man ambled over to the car. Norton pulled his window down and asked him where Patty's street was.

"What number you lookin for?" the man asked.

Norton told him.

It immediately clicked with the man. "Oh yeah," he said, "that's where all the kids live. You one of the fathers?"

Norton was uncomfortable. How did a gas station attendant know the number of the house? What was going on there? Drug busts? Orgies? Loud rock music? If Norton had been one of the fathers, would the man start telling him about the "goings-on of those kids?" Norton grunted and shook his head, answering neither yes nor no to the man's question.

The man started to give Norton directions while Norton watched his eyes very carefully, trying to ascertain what this fuck was really thinking. He had a sudden urge to drive the car over the bastard's toes. Sure, put his foot on the pedal and run the car right over the son of a bitch's feet, and then get out of the car and walk over to the prick, who would be prostrate and moaning on the dirty oil-soaked concrete, point a finger at him and say, "You watch what the fuck you're thinking next time, you lecherous old bastard! Just because you'd like to get a little of that young stuff yourself, you think that's all I'm after, huh? You knew I wasn't one of the fathers—you were just trying to get me up tight. You're jealous, right? You see these pretty young kids and you'd like to do what you think I'm doing? Right?" The man wouldn't be answering; he would just be moaning and holding his toes. And Norton would walk back to the car.

Triumphant!

Meanwhile, Norton had missed one of the directions.

"Is that the second right?" he asked the man.

"No, the third," the man replied. "Can't miss it, big Mobil station on the corner."

"Thank you," Norton said, rolling up his window and watching the man out of the corner of his eye and then from his rear-view mirror to see if the man would be sauntering up to the other attendant to start gossiping about him. But the attendant was out of his sight before he could discern anything, and Norton concentrated on getting to the third right and spotting the Mobil Station.

A few minutes later he came to the house and parked not quite in front of it so that he could look it over. The house was very quiet—no loud rock music blaring from the windows. A very ordinary old American home, he thought. How did it get known by someone like that gas station attendant? Was it just because there were a bunch of kids with long hair in a staid old New England town, conjuring up all kinds of drug and sex images in the superstitious local unconscious?

Patty wouldn't be involved with any of that. Maybe a little pot once in a while, but no heavy drugs for her. As for sex orgies, well, forget that—he knew her too well.

Then what was it?

Ahh, one of the kids must have tried to commit suicide, that's what must have happened. That's why the house was known. These kids are always trying to commit suicide.

Relieved at having found the answer, he emerged from the car, at once feeling out of place because of the way he was dressed. Light summer beige business suit, green striped tie —totally inappropriate for this occasion.

I look like a father or a businessman on the make, he told himself as he hastily removed his jacket and tie.

He hoped no one was watching him as he changed his image, so to speak, feeling they would be thinking he was a phony.

I'm not being a phony. I'm just getting comfortable. It's a hot summer night, he found himself explaining to those secret, young, skeptical eyes.

The weight that he was putting on was beginning to show in the roll at his midsection, and his shirt was dirty, wrinkled, very unattractive. Patty would be repelled.

He hastily put on his jacket and unbuttoned the second button from the top of his shirt, allowing the curly hair on his chest to show.

Yes, he thought, looking at himself, gives me kind of a sporty casual look that's just right.

He walked quickly to the house and knocked on the door. He heard a sound in the house and braced himself for the surprised look on Patty's face when she saw him. As the door started to open he became frightened at what she would do. Would she slam the door in his face? Not let him in?

It was not Patty.

It was an ugly young girl with deep, suspicious eyes and a pimply face.

He was the one with a surprised look on his face as the young lady stood there waiting for him to say what he wanted.

"Yes?" she asked. There was immediate hostility from the girl.

He cleared his throat, but when his voice came out it was way up there again, damn it.

"Is Patty home?"

"No," the girl replied, just staring at him, not offering anything more.

"Oh," Norton said, and just stood there, waiting for more information.

This girl is a lesbian, Norton suddenly knew. She is after my Patty—maybe she already has her. Once a sweet little thing like Patty gets in the grip of a butch bitch like this they're almost impossible to rescue. They learn to hate men.

Oh, Donald, his fat-ass voice said, you're not a moment too soon. Press on—press on.

"Where can I find her?" he asked.

"I don't really know," the butch bitch said. He could tell she was well-educated, sharp and intelligent.

"I'd like to find her," Norton persisted.

"Are you her father?"

"No," Norton said quickly. Was that it? This butch bitch thought he was Patty's crazy father—is that why she was so unfriendly? Norton felt warmly relieved when, after the girl looked him over carefully, as if to check if there were any resemblance between him and Patty, she said to him in a friendlier way, "Come in."

Norton stepped into the house.

"Wait here," she said, touching his arm reassuringly and walking into another room.

Oh, Donald, what a nice girl, fat-ass was saying.

Oh, yes, fat-ass, isn't she lovely? he replied.

Probably a loving, warm companion for your little darling. And you were so suspicious, silly boy.

The girl came back quickly.

"She's probably at Lonnie's," she said. "That's a bar around three miles down the road to the east. Which way is your car facing?"

He indicated that it was facing on the right of the road and she said, "Fine. Just continue down the road and you'll see it on the right."

What a kind little girl. Ask her her name, Donald.

"What's your name?" Norton asked.

"Ginny," the girl replied.

Now pat her head and show her that you think she is a nice little girl, and reach into your pocket and give her some money for being so helpful, fat-ass directed.

Stop that! he commanded.

Ginny had the eerie feeling for a moment that this strange but good-looking man with the wide, dazed eyes and the high, young-boy voice was about to reach out and touch her. She cringed slightly, stepped back and started to think about what to do if it happened.

Instead, the man stammered, "Thank you," turned away and walked quickly to his car. Before stepping into his car he turned around and waved to her, smiling in a friendly way, and she waved back, wondering as she closed the door and went back to her room what the hell this was all about.

Lonnie's was a roadside bar in the middle of a rocky dirt parking lot. Norton sat in the parking lot watching people go in and out of the bar—young people with dirty blue jeans as uniforms—all belonging there as naturally as trees in a forest. He hated the idea of walking in, and hoped that Patty would take a stroll outside. But as he waited he knew that it was unlikely to happen that way and that he would probably have to go inside.

He saw a man go into the bar who no doubt was even older than Norton. The man had graying hair and was paunchy and wearing an older man's sport jacket and slacks, no blue jeans. The man was walking in naturally, as if he belonged there, and this encouraged Norton. He stepped out of the car and approached the bar door. As he was about to open the door he had the frightening feeling that his entrance would cause everyone at the bar to stop what they were doing and stare at him like in some bad Western movie.

He opened the door and went in quickly, his mouth dry and his eyes searching for a place to position himself as inconspicuously as possible. He was in a large, dimly lit smokey room with a big bar in the center. No one looked up or seemed to care if he was there or not. So far so good. Should he look around for Patty? No, not yet. Land first. Secure a safe harbor and then reconnoiter. Don't look around. Someone will think you are a cop and come up and try to hit you. You don't want trouble. Patty will laugh at you if you get beaten up. After this is over, take lessons. Yes. Kung Fu. Karate. Boxing. All of it. You can afford it now. Then you can walk into any place and not give a shit for anyone. Yes. Knock 'em on their ass if they fuck with you!

He was at the bar and there was a beer in front of him, handed to him upon his request by a bored young bartender. He sipped the beer, waiting until he blended in with the surroundings before he dared look around to try to locate Patty.

Suddenly he felt deeply depressed. This wasn't the kind of place she would be in. He knew it. She had left decoy instructions with that butch bitch Ginny. She really did not want to see him any more in any way, shape or form. She didn't want to talk to him. He knew it. And he sank deeper and deeper into his terrible depression, body rankling with pain, buzzing with anxiety.

Then he saw her, to his right. She was with five or six young people at a distant table. She was smoking a cigarette and drinking a drink, talking and laughing and being very relaxed. As he saw her again he marveled at how pretty she was. In the smoke and gloom of this bar she sat there glowing and no one seemed to pay any special attention to her. Why didn't everyone at the bar stop what they were doing and just stare at this pretty glowing creature? Why did these fools just treat her presence as ordinary and commonplace?

Oh, you're such a romantic, Donald.

He had never seen her this way before—relaxed, talking, laughing; and so he just studied her awhile. She was going to be with him a long time now and he wanted to get to know her, her every move, her every gesture. He heard her laugh and it was a giddy, high, girlish laugh. She was young, there was no denying that, but even in her youth he could discern her poise, her grace, her warm charm. Was he choosing right? he asked himself as he looked her over. Is this really my soul mate? My love? Yes. Yes, of course it was. There could be no doubt about it. Donald, press on—press on, fat-ass said.

He took his beer and moved to the end of the bar close to her table and sat there, now ready for her to see him.

There were two boys and four girls at the table. The boys looked like farm boys—silly stupid yokel-looking kids, and the girls looked very young, almost like high school girls. Was she with one of the boys? She could be but it wouldn't mean anything. How could one of those young yokels be any competition for someone like him? Was it the one with the overalls and sandy hair that was after her? Did he want her to go to bed with him? It's not so easy for her, you dumb jerk. She needs love, warmth, understanding and insight. All you've got to offer her is your pimply adolescent panting. Keep away from her, don't try to confuse her.

How was he going to let her know that he was there? If he went to the table and made his presence known, wouldn't it cause a scene? Yes, yes it might. If she didn't want to see him it would be doubly awful in front of her friends. He could imagine them trying to hide their laughter at the sight of this older man being rejected by one of their own kind—revenge on the older generation—everyone in the bar laughing at him, laughing silently with their eyes, waiting for him to leave so they could talk and laugh out loud about him over their beers.

He looked around the bar and at the other end he thought he saw the gas station attendant he had met before.

He wanted to leave—get in the car—get back on the highway—get home—get into bed—go to sleep—tired of all this anxiety—tired of all these fears and walking nightmares. If he left now it might still be all right. He knew there was something wrong. He knew that the course he had been following lately might not be the right course. Perhaps he ought step back a moment before he went further. Open up more with Claude. Admit that he had had an affair with a patient. Claude wouldn't arrest him or have him defrocked (we psychiatrists are the modern priests, are we not?). He laughed at his use of the word "defrocked"—it ought to be "deFreuded," he thought.

But her prettiness and the sense of the times they were together were just enough to nudge away any thoughts of not having her again.

He stared at her intensely, willing her to look at him.

Look up and to your right, he commanded her.

Look up and see me.

Look up.

She saw him in the middle of a laugh. He enjoyed how her eyes widened ever so slightly and how she just trailed the laugh off, not making anything conspicuous. She politely excused herself from the others, moved out from behind the table and walked over to him at the bar.

"Hello, Donald," she muttered.

He just nodded and they stood there side by side for a while.

"You shocked me just now," she finally said.

"You didn't look or act shocked," he replied. Thank God his voice sounded all right. He felt calm. He could handle it.

"You know how I hide my feelings."

He half laughed.

"Can we go outside and talk or something?"

"I—I'm with my friends . . ." she said.

"Oh," he replied, and just waited there.

"Well, just for a little bit. Then I have to get right back. We're going someplace."

"Sure," he said, very reasonably.

She quickly went back to the table and said something to her friends. He turned away and finished his beer, not wanting to face the inquiring furtive stares that he knew her friends would be directing at him.

She came back, touched his arm and he followed her out into the parking lot.

They just walked a bit side by side.

He really did not know what to say.

After all, in their sessions she had always started all the talking.

"How have you been?" she finally said.

"Oh, I've been all right. How have you been, Patty? Have you been in control?"

How he hated what he sounded like: analytical, pompous, removed—all the qualities that she had run away from.

She looked sharply at him. Would she say what she was feeling? Would she say, "Cut out that psychological shit, Donald. What are you here for?" He almost wished she would.

Instead she said, "I've been doing fine."

He swallowed hard and looked at her in a quick sideward glance. "I miss you."

"Thank you," she replied, a polite little girl receiving a compliment. He could almost imagine her curtsying.

He abruptly stood in front of her, halting them. She caught her breath slightly because of the suddenness of the movement and looked directly at him, her lips parted to say something in protest. But the words never came out, because in his eyes she saw a directness and an intensity that had never been there before. For the first time since she had known him and had let him make love to her he seemed to be looking into the middle of her, needing her in a way she had never seen, or felt, before.

"I miss you very much," he said. Then he took her by the arms and kissed her on the lips, first lightly, and when she didn't pull away, with greater intensity.

She let the cigarette drop from her hands and put her arms around him and held him tightly, boring into his mouth in quick abandon of all her resolution.

"Darling . . . darling . . ." he muttered. "I love you . . . I love you . . ."

She stiffened.

He felt the marvelous surge of warmth slowly ebb from her as he held her in his arms and kissed her more fervently than before, anxiously trying to revive the warmth. But the stiffness flowed into her body very quickly now and he could only let her go.

She walked on ahead of him and he followed her.

"Patty . . . wait . . . stop."

She stopped.

He stopped behind her.

"I know what you're thinking," he said. Analytical position, he noted. Doctor behind patient. Patient facing away from doctor. Doctor interpreting patient's actions. No good. No more of that. Get in front of her.

He moved in front of her. But she turned away. Patient more comfortable in more familiar position.

"How could you know what I am thinking?" she said.

"I'm your psychiatrist, am I not? At least I was . . . of

143

course I know what you're thinking, and I don't blame you."

"Oh?" she said.

Is she getting angry? Her back seemed to straighten when she said that. Anger would be good here—now. She needs to get at her anger or we won't be able to get anywhere. He must help her.

"You must be thinking," he said, "that I'm saying that I love you to . . . to . . . you know . . . for the convenience of the moment, right?"

She did not answer.

"I don't blame you. I really don't. It would be impossible for anyone to feel otherwise." God, stop sounding so damn pompous again! Remember what happened just before when you were real, when you really told her that you missed her. Be real again.

"I've thought about it endlessly since you've gone away. I've thought about you endlessly. I—I really love you."

She turned and looked at him briefly, then started to walk again, not ahead of him this time but letting him walk side by side with her.

"I wasn't thinking that, Donald," she said after a while. There were tears in her eyes as she stared straight ahead.

"I was thinking how badly I wanted to tell you that I loved you during all that time, and how frightened I was of doing it . . ."

The tears started to come more rapidly. She took a tissue from her jeans and started to dab her eyes and nose.

"I—I didn't know if I was supposed to tell you that or even if I was supposed to feel it . . ."

She stopped and he took her by the shoulders and brought her head to rest on his chest, gently kissing her hair.

"You're supposed to say what you feel, you little character. And you can't control how you feel." He could teach her so much.

He gently hugged her to let her know that he wanted to

teach her, that he would take care of her, see to it that she would not feel that her feelings were prisoners.

"And now you've decided that you love me?"

Her voice was different now. Norton said nothing. He became wary. She moved away from him. The tears were no longer there and she looked directly at him.

"All those times I didn't know what was happening. I came to you every week—with us looking at each other the way we did. It scared me so much and still I couldn't wait for each session. But I was still having all those problems— my father, boys, school. Even so, all I could do was just look at you and wait. Wait for what? I didn't even dare tell myself what I was waiting for. And then you made love to me and after that I thought I would be happy, but then I was even more unhappy, but each week I still looked forward to seeing you. And all this time my father was driving me crazy and I couldn't concentrate on school, and boys . . . boys, I just couldn't cope with what they wanted. What the hell were you doing to me, Donald? What were you *doing* to me?"

She's getting it out, he thought, a year ago before she came into treatment with me she never could have said these things to anyone. Look at her—face flushed—eyes flaming— totally beautiful in her anger! What I saw in her is there! She is an absolutely marvelous person!

"And now you've decided that you love me?" she continued. She walked up very close to him and whispered vehemently, "Did you love me while you were fucking me, Donald?"

Yes, get it out.

"Did you? Did you love me while you were fucking me? Answer me, doctor!"

"Yes. Yes. I loved you but I wasn't aware that I did."

"Oh, now you are aware. How nice. Do you know what love is, doctor? If you loved me, why didn't you send me to someone else and see me like a man and a woman? Why didn't you try to help me solve some of my problems?"

"I did . . . I tried . . . in my way I tried . . . you know I did . . . but look, the truth is, I was caught up in something I didn't entirely understand until now—"

"Bullshit! You were just a married man playing around."

"No. I loved you."

"You are the same kind of shit as my father, who will fuck anything he can get his hands on, at the same time carrying on when he finds birth control pills in the drawer where his daughter keeps her underthings. . . . I wonder what he was doing there in the first place."

All of these accusations were handleable. Given time, he could let her know that he wasn't really like that, but would he have the time? She would soon run out of fury and recrimination and storm away and be lost to him forever. She was looking back now toward the bar, and he could almost hear her thinking about what she was going to say to him in parting. She would be polite, contrite, wish him luck and get away as quickly as possible.

"I want to do that now," he said.

"Do what now?"

"See you," he said, looking directly at her, holding her skeptical stare in his eyes.

"What do you mean?" Patty said.

"I want to see you like . . . like a man and a woman. I want to date you." He had almost said "court."

She lit another cigarette and leaned against a nearby car. He leaned near her, his elbow on the roof of the car, studying her thin lips as they exhaled the smoke.

"I suppose we can pick out a nice motel somewhere between here and New York where we could meet once a week?" she asked softly.

He didn't answer. He was wary.

"I wouldn't want to get back too late because I have to

get up early, and I guess you don't want to get home too late either, do you?"

"I don't want that."

"What?"

"What you're describing. I don't want that."

"Oh? What do you want?"

"I'm not with my wife any more."

"Oh, really."

"I told you that, remember?"

"I must have forgotten. Look, I have to get back soon," she said, looking nervously at the bar door to see if any of her friends were looking for her.

"Patty, I love you."

"Thank you," she said. "I know how it feels. I've loved you too."

He moved close to her and softly kissed her.

"Loved?"

"Yes, loved," she said firmly.

"Patty, I'm going to get a divorce. I love you. I want to marry you."

The words seemed to slice the air.

They hit home.

She slowly turned and looked at him. This awesome, handsome, strange, brilliant man who had been so much in her life for so long was saying that all this time he had not been just using her . . . was saying that he had loved her. She had not been just a little plaything for him . . . this new strange intensity . . . this coming here to see her and now this talking about marriage—seeing, believing her value to him made her feel good . . . valuable herself. As her raging hypocrite of a father could never do. . . . It wasn't his proposal—it was his honest need. That filled her, freed her.

And now she could give him what he wanted so badly. She could take him in her arms and move close to him and give him what he so obviously needed.

She wrapped her arms tightly around him and brought him close to her.

He put his arms around her, and for a while they just stood there like that, quietly, against a parked Chevrolet.

He bent down to kiss her—kiss his future wife—the person who was going to make him totally happy. She returned his kiss, pressing herself into him without any holding back.

He felt himself getting aroused, felt his erection catapulting up, and he moved his body slightly away from her so that she wouldn't feel it—wouldn't think that that was all he wanted.

She wondered why he pulled away, not minding the feeling of his sex now because she knew that she was more than that to him . . . wanting to tell him that he could have her if he wanted right here, right now, if that would make him happy, if that would relieve that awful intensity she saw in him.

"It won't take me long to get a divorce," he said. He was compelled to talk about marriage. He had to hear what she would say.

He felt Patty tense ever so slightly again, as if she didn't want to hear him talk any more.

But he had to hear what she would say! "There won't be any long legal battles, you'll see," he continued.

Patty put her mouth on his lips and kissed him ferociously, moving her body fiercely into his, wanting to feel his erection pressed against her stomach, wanting to feel his hands on her breasts. He pulled his head away from the kiss and looked into her closed eyes. "We'll live wherever you like," he whispered to her eyes, waiting for them to open up and wanting her to talk about marriage. Her eyes wouldn't open. She kissed his face fervently.

"If you like this country living, we'll live in the country; if you like the city, we'll live in the city. I can practice anywhere. It doesn't matter to me as long as I have you."

Oh God, what is all this he's saying! Can't he stop talking that way, can't he just make love to me and make himself happy, relieve himself?

She became determinedly wanton in her effort to silence this flood of impossible, jumbled words. She ground herself into him until the erection she now felt almost seemed to come from her. His hands mercifully went to the sides of her breasts. She was ready to make love—here and now—up against a parked car—in a back seat—anywhere, with total abandon. Wouldn't her psychiatrist be proud of her? She could have an orgasm now. She could be free with her body.

"Patty, let's stop now. I want to let you know that I mean everything I say about marriage. I don't want you to think that I'm saying it just because I want you. We won't do anything more until we're married. You'll see that I really love you. After we're married, darling, there'll be plenty of time."

"Stop this phony talk about marriage," she whispered, wrenching herself away from him and leaning against the parked car, breathing hard, somehow feeling used again the same way as in the sessions, looking now at the door of the bar and wondering if her friends might be getting worried about her.

She was wanting to go in again, he noticed, relieved that no beckoning friend was nearby.

"Patty," he said, moving close to her turned back, "I was being silly. Forgive me—it's just that I thought I was going to lose you. I know it's ridiculous to talk about marriage now."

"I'm not ready for marriage, Donald," she said. "You should know that better than anyone else. I'm not ready for any long-standing relationship. I—I just want to hang out for a while and take things loose and get the feeling of living away from home and not get into anything too heavy—"

"Hey, yeah, sure, that's cool."

She laughed at his use of slang. "Oh, Donald."

"Cool, baby," he continued, delighted that he had made her laugh.

He put his arm around her shoulders. They started to walk slowly back to the bar.

"We'll date," he said casually, "it's not too long from New York to here. I'll come up on weekends—some weekdays too if you like—I can arrange it, nothing heavy, everything cool."

She said nothing and they walked a few more paces.

"How about this Saturday? Maybe we could go to a movie and eat out. You know, this is the first time I've seen you outside of the office."

She still wasn't saying anything.

"I like the way we walk together," he continued. "I like the way we fit together. I mean, I'm not too old for you, am I? I'm only forty. That's not too ancient, is it? I know lots of people more than twenty years apart in age who do quite well."

"Donald," she finally said.

He waited.

"I—I had decided that I wasn't going to see you any more."

They stopped walking.

"I thought about it a lot and I think it's really best for me if I don't see you any more."

"I knew you'd be thinking that," he said. He knew that she had to be taught, but he knew, had just before received the evidence of it, that she could be taught. Look how she had just responded!

"You've helped me a lot, you really did. You taught me a lot—"

"Do you know why you're doing this?" he asked. "I mean why—really why?"

"I—I just want to go out with boys . . . people my own age, starting out the way I am."

"Those are rationalizations, Patty, not reasons. I know the

reasons, and unless you deal with them you won't get anywhere. You'll form a pattern that you'll never break, patterns
that will strangle you. I will help you break these strangle-
holds with love and understanding and insight—insight,
Patty, trained, incisive insight!"

"Please, Donald."

"You don't want to face what really happened. You were
beginning to come alive, beginning to respond to me with
your entire body, your entire being was beginning to open
up. The last time we made love, remember that? Remember
that? You were alive, you had never been like that. Patty, I
know what happened, I was a fool not to predict it. You
became frightened, subconsciously frightened. You did not
want to respond because you had been taught that responding was bad. You were being a bad girl. You did something
to disrupt your own progress—think—think about what you
must have done to cause your father to find those birth control pills and start that argument that led to your leaving
home . . . leaving us."

She mumbled something that he didn't hear.

He asked her to repeat it.

Looking down and away from him, she said, "Donald, I'm
going with somebody now."

The words knifed into him. His head felt slammed from
the inside and his capillaries were popping and doing a
dance of death within him.

"Oh—" He tried to get his bearings, stopping and leaning
casually against a parked car, bending down to tie a shoe-
lace. She stopped too, and became occupied with the lace.

"These damn laces," he muttered while he tied it.

She nodded in agreement about the damn laces.

He retied the other one.

"Nothing heavy," she said. "But I just want to see him and
not anyone else for a while."

Norton gestured slightly toward the bar with his head.

"One of those . . . ?" he trailed off, wanting to know which of the two young men it was, yet not knowing what to call any of her male friends. He couldn't call them "boys" because how could he, Dr. Donald Norton, be in love with a girl who went with "boys"? "Chap" was too stiff, so was "young man," and "guy" sounded too inappropriate for kids like those two . . . two kids in the bar.

Which one of them is her boy friend?

Had she been to bed with him yet?

It certainly didn't take her long, did it?

She sure gets around, doesn't she?

He wanted to whip those things at her—hurt her, put her on the defensive. He wanted to ask her how she thought her new boy friend would feel if he had seen how she was behaving with him just a few minutes ago.

"No," she said. "He's not one of those boys with me at the table. I'm seeing him later."

Quickly it became important that he show her how concerned he had been for her welfare. He was grateful that he was aware enough to check his anger and not do or say anything that would be irretrievable.

"Someone about your own age?" he asked.

"He's nineteen."

"Oh, a little bit younger than you."

She nodded and started to walk back to the bar again. He followed at her side—slowing the pace, trying to delay the moment that she would disappear into the bar.

"Goes to college, does he?" Norton asked.

"No," she replied. "He works in a gas station."

The knife twisted in him more. If it had only been a brilliant young college boy, a budding doctor, a lawyer or even a sharp young business executive.

"A mechanic?" he asked.

"No, he just takes care of customers and things like that."

The worst of it was that she did not seem to be defensive or ashamed of her new lover's status. She was a college girl, brought up in a good family with a good degree of intelligence. What the hell was she doing to herself!

"Are you in love with him?" he asked.

"I—I don't know . . . I don't think I know what love is . . ."

"Well, you should have some idea . . . should know whether or not your new choice is valid and healthy. The way you responded to me before, does that happen with him?"

"Donald, please."

"Have you been to bed with him yet? I—I'm just asking to get some idea of the nature of the relationship."

"Please . . ."

"Have you?"

"No, not yet," she said softly, looking away. "He wants me to but I haven't yet."

"I see," he said, relieved, able to press on now. "You were ready to make love to me before, weren't you?"

"No."

"Don't say that to me, Patty. I felt what you were feeling. If I had taken you in my car or in the woods or against a car—"

"Stop."

"Admit the truth!"

"All right."

"So we have the fact that you were ready to make love to the man you are trying to get rid of—and may I say more than ready—you were as soft and free as an alive vital person should be . . ." He came closer to her, held her as if his holding her would make her see the truth of his wisdom. "And you cannot bring yourself to make love to this new person you have chosen. You can't make love to him because you are acting out your fears and sublimating your feelings. I must make you see that!"

"Donald," she said, "I would have made love to you before, but not because I love you or want to be with you again."

"You're rationalizing, you're hiding."

"No." She interrupted him strongly. She swallowed and took a short deep breath. "You see, up until that moment I just thought of myself as something you used. I worshipped you, and the only time we could have together was the fifty minutes once a week that my father paid for. And now here you were talking to me about love and marriage and looking at me so intensely and . . . and I don't know, I wasn't just a little groupie any more, waiting to be fondled by the big-doctor rock star. I was worthwhile. I could feel like me and I could offer *that*."

God, he had done a good job with this girl. Here she was looking at him, telling him this, being very real and very simple. What she was saying was the end of him and he knew it, but the simple nobility of what she was saying and how she was saying it moved him in a way that he had never been moved before. He could only listen now, not argue.

"I won't see you again, Donald, but thank you for coming up here." She put her hand on his arm and squeezed it softly. "Don't ruin it, don't press me."

He leaned against the porch of the bar. She did too.

"Will you be all right?" he asked.

She nodded. "I'll be all right. Will you?"

"Sure, I have a good psychiatrist."

"I didn't know you went to one too."

"I never told you?"

"No."

"Well, I do."

"Do you listen to what he tells you?"

"Not always."

They laughed.

"You were beautiful just now, you know that?" he told her.

"You're being beautiful now," she said.

They smiled at each other.

"I have to go now."

"If you need a referral to any other psychiatrist up around

here I'll be glad to help you find the best one available."

She thought a moment. "No," she said. "It'll be a long time before I'll be able to go to . . . to someone again."

She half turned and walked up the steps. He wanted to tell her that if she was ever in the city to give him a call, but he found that he could not talk.

As he watched her going up the steps he told himself that it was apparent that it was all inappropriate now. She was merely a child . . . a child with emotional problems. It could never have worked and it was so much better that it turned out this way. God, what if she had listened to all that stuff about marriage? He was lucky, really, lucky this thing hadn't gone any further than it did. He would be strong and calm now. He would really get to work with Claude and go into the whole thing and learn so much about himself. He would be strong and calm—strong and calm. The moment that she was no longer in sight—the moment that she disappeared back into the bar would be the moment of birth of the inner tranquillity that he so fervently was pursuing. Like a ray of sublime light in a holy picture, great inner peace and tranquillity would flow into him and he would forever be strong and calm. Strong and calm.

Patty walked into the bar without turning around.

Strong and calm.

Strong and calm.

At peace . . . like Peter . . .

chapter ten

HE drove back into the city, down to Greenwich Village, where he looked up the address of the acting school that Carmelita and Peter attended. He found it on a quiet street in the West Village and was able to park his car opposite the entrance.

This was the night that they had their acting class, and, as he recalled from her mentioning it one session, the class should be over soon.

He could not sit in the car and wait, so he stepped out and waited on the sidewalk, leaning against an apartment building. The night had gotten chilly and he was cold, so he huddled as close to the brick wall as he could, preferring the bite of the weather to the safe but tomblike insulation of his car.

In a few minutes a group of exuberant people emerged from the studio—obviously actors and actresses, mostly young. They seemed very loud, showy. They became a maze of noise, Afro hairdos, beards and blue jeans. There was no Carmelita among them at first, and he was trying to focus on which individual in the maze he would choose to ask about her, when she came out of the studio.

Next to her, deep in conversation, was, of course, Peter.

He was as she described him: short, slim with a Buster Brown haircut, glasses, and seemingly asleep on his feet. Yet in his walk there was a litheness that made Carmelita's contention of his power on stage easily believable.

Norton watched them walk by him, wondering if Carmelita noticed that it was he leaning there against the building.

Her eyes took him in at a glance but did not pause even a second. Of course to her the possibility that her revered psychiatrist would be outside her acting school, huddled against an apartment house wall, would never occur.

But as they passed by, Carmelita instinctively took Peter's arm and held it, as if to possess and protect her little baby against the onslaught that was to follow. Even though she did not recognize him consciously she must have perceived who he was on an unconscious level—known why he had come here tonight, sensed that he and she were to battle over Peter, and was girding herself for that battle.

Well, he would get himself ready too!

He would put on his armor for battle. No, he would take off his armor. Fling off his inhibitions. Let it, as they said, all hang out.

For a moment he wondered why he was doing this for someone he didn't even know.

But it was exactly that that made the act so powerful.

To act symbolically, without any selfish motive at all, will have the greatest impact on mankind.

But who would know what he was doing besides the people involved?

No one.

And that made it even greater.

No self-serving publicity.

A complete sacrifice of self to act symbolically.

Jesus Christ.

Jesus could have lived, but he chose to act symbolically. Jesus was riddled with neurosis before the crucifixion. Jesus must have known that by acting symbolically he would save himself. And he did. He worked through all his neuroses starting with the first spike into his flesh. To act symbolically and selflessly is the greatest piece of selfishness in the end. It is divine selfishness. With the phrase "divine selfishness" resounding through his mind, he pursued the crowd of actors down the block.

The delicious fun of it all overcame him.

He fell in right in back of Carmelita and joyfully imitated her waddle. There he was, doing it—and they all walked on without knowing he was there—and it was great. He was really good at the imitation of her walk. One would have thought he was her shadow.

Oh, how he had wanted to do things like this when he was a boy—make the grotesques of the world know how they really looked—make them see themselves in him as their mirror, and by showing them how they really were, make them stop being grotesque.

Oh, but little boy genius must never act that way!

A tall skinny actor with a fuzzy Afro who was walking next to Peter turned around and saw Norton walking behind Carmelita. The actor tapped Peter on the arm and indicated that Peter ought to look around and see what was behind him.

Peter turned and stopped, meeting the wide-eyed, gleeful gaze of Norton.

"Hey, man," Peter said, his eyes widening just a bit, "what is it?"

"Hello, Peter," Norton said—aha, his voice sounded just right.

Carmelita stopped and turned around. She looked squarely at Norton and Norton looked squarely at her.

He opened his hands in a sort of show-business gesture, as if to say, "Well, here I am, in person."

She suddenly recognized who he was and he delightedly watched her turn into all O's.

Her eyes became O's.

Her mouth became a hot pink O.

Her ears seemed to flap like an elephant's and they became O's.

To him she became one big O encircling other O's. Her nostrils, flaring Os. Her breasts. Her torso. Her handbag. Her bulbous toes.

All O's.

Norton hooked a magic string on to the round bow on top of her head and floated her away—a balloon containing other balloons.

She even gasped a short, "Oh."

"Oh," he repeated. Loving it.

"Oh," she said louder now, more aware of the horror of what she was seeing.

"Oh!" he shouted, jumping. "Yes, oh! Oh! Go-O! Go-O!"

Peter, seeing what effect this strange Village nut was having on Carmelita, asked her what was wrong as the actor with the Afro came over to Norton and said, "Take a walk, man."

Norton went into a boxer's shuffle. He shifted his weight from one foot to another, jabbed the air with a couple of left hooks, crossed with a right and laughingly sneered at the dumbfounded actor, who was looking at him and wondering what to do about this mental case.

Peter took the actor's arm and whispered something to him. Norton's identity, no doubt.

They were all staring at him now. Six big O's—no, eight, counting Peter's glasses.

Norton abruptly stopped shuffling and walked to Peter with his hands extended.

"Hello, Peter," he said, "glad to meet you. I'm Dr. Norton."

Peter limply held out his own hand and Norton shook it mock-professionally. Norton turned to get a formal introduction to the tall actor with the Afro, but as he did so the actor walked away from the three of them and proceeded slowly down the street, looking back and shaking his head as he walked.

"Are you shocked?" he asked Peter.

"No, man," Peter replied. "Why should I be shocked?"

"Good. Some people would be, you know . . ." He glanced sideways at the still mesmerized Carmelita. "Some people do not realize that we psychiatrists are just like anybody else. We walk, we talk, we stroll down streets, we box, we do imitations. She thinks we're perfect but we're not. We don't know everything."

He faced Carmelita squarely.

"Miss McKay, I am afraid I have to tell you that you don't know everything either. You were wrong about Patty. You were wrong about all that true-love stuff. I knew it all along . . . I really did, but I thought I'd give it a try anyway." Norton turned back to Peter. "She was wrong."

"Wrong . . . ?" Carmelita managed to say.

"Come, let me buy you and Peter some drinks and I'll explain the whole thing to you. Let's go to that bar you always talk about—you know, the one you go to all the time after your acting class. Drinks are on me, pardner."

Carmelita had recovered somewhat.

"Dr. Norton, are you all right?" she asked.

"Certainly," he answered. "I admit this is a bit unorthodox and you must forgive my cutting up a moment ago—must be the Village air."

"Certainly . . ." she said, obviously happy to believe that the entire scene was just a delusion.

"I wanted to talk to you both. Is that all right? No charge," he said.

"Sure," Peter answered.

Norton moved in between them, put his arms around their shoulders and they all started to walk.

Norton saw Peter smiling and trying to catch Carmelita's eye. Carmelita had her head turned away and was walking stiffly. She did not want to look at Peter.

"What are you thinking, Peter?" Norton asked.

"Nothing much."

"Bet I know."

Peter laughed nervously.

"I bet you're thinking: 'Is this the guy that she wanted me to go to?' Is that what you're thinking, Peter? Is that why you're trying to catch her eye, huh?"

Peter laughed harder and Norton laughed with him. "Maybe," Peter said.

Norton turned to Carmelita. "And you, my dear . . . are you embarrassed? Are you angry at me?"

"No . . . no . . ." Carmelita said, "I know . . . I'm sure that whatever you do . . . you must have something constructive in mind . . ."

They had reached the bar.

Norton stopped and looked deeply at her.

"You are so good. Kind. Considerate. Loving. So free from scornful anger."

He watched her eyes as they almost lit up, almost became fired by these words of approval from someone so important to her. But then she snuffed the flame, stiffened herself and shook her head as if to shake the images of what she was seeing out of her mind and have them burst like bubbles on the concrete of the sidewalk.

Round O's of bubbles shooting through her ears, nose and mouth and falling to the sidewalk appeared to him as he watched her.

It was hilarious.

He laughed.

She turned around and walked into the bar. They followed her and they all sat down at a table in the back. A slim middle-aged waitress with black dyed hair came to take their order.

Norton pointed to Peter. "Whatever he wants, double it. Double everything for him and double everything for me."

The waitress looked toward Peter. "The usual?" she asked. He nodded.

"Double usual for me," Norton told her, then indicating Carmelita he said, "Cut hers in half." Turning quickly to a non-smiling Carmelita, he said, "I'm only joking. Give her anything she wants."

The waitress asked Carmelita if she wanted her usual and when Carmelita nodded, numbly, the waitress walked away.

Norton put a wad of money on the table. He spread it out like a deck of cards.

"What's happening, man?" Peter asked him. "What's it all about?"

"Money. I want to spend all this money on a good cause. This money is from fees I really didn't earn. Fees I collected when I was doing things I oughtn't to have been doing. I don't always do what I ought to do. But now I am. I really am saving someone now."

"Who are you saving?" Peter asked.

"I am earning my fee," Norton said, and took some money from the table and put it in his pocket. "It feels good to really earn your fee."

"How are you earning your fee?" Peter asked.

"I'm saving someone."

"Who are you saving?"

"You."

"Me?"

Carmelita turned sharply and listened carefully.

"I'm saving you from me. How can I help you when I am the way I am? We are all the way I am. Keep away from us."

"Dr. Norton!" Carmelita said.

"You are perfect. We should all go to you," Norton said, and he pushed all the money on the table toward Peter.

"No!" Carmelita said to Peter. "Don't listen to him. Can't you see he's sick? He's got a fever of some kind . . . he's delirious . . . Peter, let's take him home and get him some medical attention . . ."

Peter nodded in agreement.

"No . . . no, I'm not sick. I just came from a doctor this afternoon and I'm fine. Never been better in my life. Put your hand on my forehead." Norton turned to Carmelita. "Go on, put your hand on my forehead." Carmelita slowly obeyed. Her palm rested on his forehead.

"How does it feel?" he asked her.

"I don't know."

"Is it hot?"

"I can't really tell."

He was furious with her. He took her hand off his forehead and tossed it away angrily.

"You can't really tell anything, can you?"

Tears came to her eyes.

"You told me to press on . . . press on and win your own true love. And you were wrong. You think you know everything but you don't know everything. She didn't want me. And even if she had, would she have made me happy? Does true love make you happy? 'Oh, Donald, Donald, find your true love and you will find happiness' . . ."

Norton suddenly looked across the room at another table where he saw a young actress with long black hair seated with her back to him.

"Patty!" he yelled, his voice breaking the conversational hum in the bar like a gunshot. "Patty!" he yelled again, standing up. People turned around to look. The waitress stopped preparing her orders and looked back, wondering if she ought to go and quiet down this strange bird. Carmelita pulled Norton back into his seat.

"Her name is Marsha," she whispered, trying to hide her tears from all the people looking on.

"Marsha?" Norton said, still staring at the back of the girl, who had not turned around in spite of the yelling. "Pardon me, Marsha," he said across the room.

Marsha turned around and looked at Norton, wondering what was going on.

"You're not Patty," he told her. "Sorry."

She shrugged and returned to her conversation.

Carmelita was in full tears now.

"Why are you crying?"

"Doctor, please let us take you somewhere ... Peter, let's take him home."

"Where do you live, man?" Peter asked.

"Am I embarrassing you?" Norton asked them.

"I'm not embarrassed," Peter said.

Carmelita said nothing.

"Are you embarrassed?" Norton asked Carmelita. "Come on, you can tell me the truth. I won't be angry if you tell me that I am embarrassing you."

She nodded her head, not trusting herself to speak or to look at him.

"Well, you see, that is a problem I can help you with. There is no need for you to be embarrassed by anything I do. I'm not your father. You were embarrassed when your father was drunk in public. I know that ... but this is different. I am on a mission now. A selfless holy mission. I want to save Peter and, you know what? I think I'll save you too. You're not such a bad sort after all."

"Doctor, please let us take you home."

"No . . . no, listen, gather close to me because I am going to give you the secret. People always think we have the secret and they are right—we do. Peter, listen to this. I'm going to give you the secret."

He dropped his voice in a conspiratorial whisper, and in spite of themselves Peter and Carmelita gathered very close to him.

"There is no such thing as true happiness. True love is a myth. We psychiatrists know that. We know it from the beginning, but we don't let on, because if we told everyone, then they wouldn't come to us. We couldn't make a living. So I tell you don't look for the love in your heart, it's all a waste of time and energy. Look for the hate."

He turned to Carmelita and said sharply to her: "How do you feel about me now?"

"I want to help you."

"Why?"

"Oh, doctor, please . . ."

"You want to help me because you see me as a suffering human being in need of compassion, right?"

"Yes."

"You love your fellow man and want to help him in his time of need, right?"

"Yes."

"You don't hate me because I have embarrassed you in front of your friends . . ."

"No. You are not well."

"So you feel nothing but compassion toward me?"

"Yes. Oh, please, doctor, let us take you home."

"Is there anything I can tell you that would make you hate me?"

"No."

He pushed some money toward her.

"Wanna bet?" he said, a little evil-boy gleam in his eye. She became apprehensive. "What do you mean?"

"It was me who put the little mousey on the bookshelf."

Carmelita gasped. Her face turned a purply kind of red and her nostrils flared. Norton felt satisfied. He had hit home. He had proved his point.

The drinks came.

Norton picked up his glass.

"A toast to hate. This is hate. Drink the hate." He drank. He didn't like the taste. He hated the taste. That was as it should be. He hated the hate.

"Drink the hate!" he screamed to everyone in the bar.

"Hey, mister, cut it out!" the waitress said sharply to him.

"I'm sorry," Norton said. He put his head on the table, almost knocking over the glass. He at once felt deflated, a bit dizzy, unexcited and very weak.

"You're going to have to get out of here if you don't behave yourself, buddy," the waitress said.

"Donald is sorry," he murmured. "Donald has to learn to adjust to freedom. Freedom is not license, Donald."

"Well, you better tell Donald to cut it out," the waitress said.

"Don't worry," he reassured her. "I am Donald's psychiatrist. I will take care of him." He pushed some money toward her. "Here's your fee. Thank you very much."

The waitress took the money for the drinks and walked away.

He turned to Carmelita, who was shaking now, trembling with rage, he noted, yet he wondered if she knew how enraged she really was.

"Will you tell Patty to come over here. I would like to apologize for the way I've been acting lately."

Carmelita did not even hear what he said. Peter touched Norton's arm and Norton turned to Peter.

"That is not Patty. That is Marsha," he said.

"Oh." He drank his drink again. "Drink hate." He watched Peter sip his drink. He seemed so relaxed, eyes almost closed, so much at peace with himself. "Peter, tell Donald how to be perfect."

"I don't know how to be perfect, man."

"Oh, but you are perfect, only you don't know it. You sleep through the mundane shit of life and wake up only to be magnificent. That is perfect inner peace."

Peter decided to go along. "If I'm so perfect, how come I'm so unhappy?"

"Because fat-ass bugs you. She's trying to get you to adjust. Get your shit together, as you young folks say, get on lines, get work, face the world, accomplish, do, be a boy genius, achieve. That's bullshit, man. You've got it and she wants to get you away from it. Tell fat-ass to shove, and you go back to sleep and wake up only to be magnificent. That is happiness."

"No, man. That's not the way it really is. You're giving me the shit I give myself because I'm too scared. She's right. I really want to get out and work. I'm tired of just doing good work in a classroom where it doesn't really count. I want to get out there and do something in the world."

"Let me look at you," Norton said, turning Peter's shoulder around so that he could look more directly at him.

"Take your glasses off, please," he commanded easily, as if he were an intern again doing a routine exam.

Peter took his glasses off.

"Now open your eyes as wide as you can so I can see exactly what you are and what is going on."

Peter opened his eyes and Norton looked into him, and it seemed that he was able to dive through Peter's eyes into the inner pool of Peter. The water was full of electric eels slithering by, endlessly buzzing, electrifying themselves, charging the murky water with shocks and stings. And as Norton sank more deeply into the pool they slithered around him, touching him. Norton reached up and touched Peter's cheek, and through his hand he felt the little electric shocks, confirming what he by this time knew.

Peter wasn't the answer either.

This was the end.

There was no answer.

"Mama," he mumbled. "Can this really be the end?"

Peter smiled.

"Why are you smiling?"

"Dylan," Peter said.

"Dylan?"

" 'Mama, can this really be the end? To be stuck right inside of Mobile. With the Memphis Blues again.' "

Norton turned to Carmelita.

"Mama, can this really be the end," he said, and he put his arm around her shoulder. He looked up at the tears coming down her cheek and he put a finger on her cheek and a tear came down his finger. He touched the tear to his lip. And suddenly he knew the answer.

"I know where you must take me," he told them. "I've worked it through. It was there all the time and I have just seen it."

"No! We're going to take you to a hospital." Carmelita almost hissed the words at him. "A mental hospital. You are having a mental breakdown! Peter, we are going to take him to Bellevue!"

"Now you hate me. Now you are letting the anger come out. I have done a good job. I've earned my fee." He took some money off the table and put it in his pocket. "The answer for you is the anger. Work with the anger. Remember that."

"You are crazy," she told him. "Crazy!"

"I want you both to take me some place," Norton said.

"We're going to take you to Bellevue," Carmelita said. "If you don't come with us we'll have to call a policeman."

"No. Not Bellevue." Norton had everything under control now. He knew the way it would wind up and he was accepting it.

"Peter," he said. "You've been in a mental hospital, haven't you?"

Peter hesitated.

"Among friends . . . you can tell us . . . besides . . . I know . . . I could see those eels . . . those fuckin' eels would put anyone in a nut house. Peter . . ."

He leaned close to Peter.

"You'd better do something about those eels or you'll go back there again . . . I can tell. Get some treatment . . . it's all right . . . I give you my permission . . ."

"Listen, man," Peter said, "we've got to take you some place."

"You will." Norton took his wallet out and handed it to Peter. "You don't have a driver's license, do you?"

"No."

"But you can drive, of course, can't you?" he said, handing Peter the wallet, which contained his driver's license, along with the keys to his car. "The driver's license will make you me. Finish your drinks and let's go."

Carmelita and Peter looked at each other, not knowing what to do.

"Where do you want us to take you?" Peter asked.

"To my psychiatrist, of course—where else?"

Norton was sitting in the back seat while Peter was driving and Carmelita was sitting in the front next to Peter. Norton felt totally numb, and his subconscious seemed to have taken over his entire system, operating it computerlike to give directions. He was able to give perfect directions to Peter without the least bit of conscious effort.

They were about to go over the George Washington

Bridge as Norton had directed when Carmelita whispered vehemently, "Peter, stop the car. Pull over and stop the car."

Peter obeyed.

"God knows where he's taking us," she said. "Look at him. His eyes blank like that. He's gone crazy. We don't know what he's liable to do."

Peter looked back at Norton's blankness. Norton was seeing and hearing everything without giving a hint that he understood or was aware of what was going on. It was as if they were talking about someone else and he was tuning in on the lives of all three of them as an interested observer.

"The only safe thing to do is take him to Bellevue," she went on.

Norton became aware of the button that locked his car door. Of course he would leap from the car if they decided to take him to Bellevue. But they wouldn't. Peter would be strong. He knew that.

"No," Peter said quietly. "I know what those places are. I'm going to take him where he wants to go."

"Peter!"

"I'm going to take him where he wants to go," Peter said firmly.

The car started again. Norton the interested observer felt that Donald the recipient of Peter's kindness ought to show Peter that he appreciated what Peter was doing for him. Norton instructed Donald to kiss Peter on the top of the head. Donald did so—softly.

They drove on over the bridge.

They drove silently from then on, the only thing said being the terse directions that Norton gave Peter. Carmelita sat throughout the entire drive frozen in anger.

Finally they pulled into Claude's driveway.

Just before the car stopped fully, Norton opened the door and jumped out. He fell and rolled over, scraping his hand. Quickly he got up and ran down the road toward the pond.

The moonlight illuminated the countryside as he ran down the road. He was free, a wild wounded animal as his brain experienced the first pain from his scraped hand. He laughed, and to his ears it sounded like the growl of an animal. He breathed hard and panted as he ran, waving his arms about, kicking high and jumping as if his two legs were hind legs. He leapt high into the air as if to meet the moon half way. When he came down he tripped and fell, rolling off the side of the road, rolling over and over again, not sure where he would land but ready to meet on its own terms any wild thing that might be there. He was stopped by the stump of a tree. He put his hand on the tree to help himself get up and he felt the stings in his hand. He pushed his hand into the wet cold dirt, welcoming the gravelly pain.

As he got up he saw the pond.

He walked slowly toward it, it drew him toward it. It wanted to draw him into its secret, and he would just let it. It wanted to give up its secret at last. It was drawing him to its invisible flow.

He heard noises behind him and without looking he knew they were searching for him with flashlights.

The pond wanted him to get down on his hands and knees and crawl into it.

The mud squished through his fingers and the water seeped through his pants as he crawled slowly into the pond. It was leading him on—bringing him further—and he went on until his body was totally immersed in the water. The pond wanted him to go below. Nothing is ever found on the surface.

He took a deep breath and dived underneath the water, his eyes open and his hands outstretched.

It was totally black as he slowly went down. He knew that his outstretched hand would find the source—the opening . . . and his hand tingled with the anticipated pleasure of the first touch of discovery. The bottom came quickly—all mud

—thick—untelling—unfeeling. He groped around. He became angry at his eyes for not helping him, so he closed them. He was running out of breath. He rose to the surface. He opened his eyes and took a deep breath and waited for the pond to draw him to its source. He saw flashlights headed down the road and voices off in the distance.

He had to work before they found him. The pond was not giving up its secrets so easily.

The sides. The source was at the sides. Of course an underground stream would come in from the side, not the bottom. He plunged down again and headed toward the side of the pond.

The sides were entwined with thick tough plants. He fought through the plants, groping along the sides of the pond—groping, pulling the plants aside—placing his hands in the mud—coming up for air and then going down again— going around the circle of the pond—around and around the circle of the pond—until he had covered it entirely.

And then it came to him that there was no source at all.

There was no beginning.

And if there was no beginning then there was no ending.

Everything was the middle.

So the pond had given him the answer.

By not having an answer it had given him the answer.

No beginning—no ending—just the middle.

Middles are very difficult to cope with. He needed help with middles.

He crawled out of the pond and sat on the muddy bank.

He looked down at himself and felt the dirt on his clothes and body.

He put his hand on his midsection and felt the roll of fat, greasy with the mud, disgusting, revolting.

He looked up and saw his analyst slowly approaching him behind a flashlight.

He stood up, brushing the dirt and mud off him as best he

could, and he walked toward his analyst to meet him half way.

When they met, Claude flicked off the flashlight and stared at his patient. And stared. And even with all his years of practiced analytical restraint, he could not keep down the sound that escaped from him, a gasp of horror and disbelief at what now stood before him.

And Norton, his voice throbbing with a lush soap opera quality, his chin doubling up and his chest expanding as if huge breasts were at that very moment growing on it, was saying, "Oh, doctor, I am so glad to meet you. I know—just know that you will be able to help me." He moved a bit closer to Claude's face, examining it as if he were seeing it for the first time, giggling flirtatiously. "You look just like a psychiatrist should look ..."